ECHO FREER

Hodder
Children's
Books

a division of Hodder Headline Limited

**To my son Jacob,
for the countless hours spent reading
the drafts of this story.**

I would like to thank the following people: Imogen Wiltshire,
Verien Wiltshire, Seema Gulati, Michael Kelly and my late
brother, Martin Freer Sunley, for providing much of the raw
material for this book.

Text copyright © 2001 Echo Freer

First published in Great Britain in 2001
by Hodder Children's Books

10 9 8 7 6 5 4 3

A Catalogue record for this book is available from
the British Library

ISBN 0 340 84148 6

Typeset by Avon Dataset Ltd, Bidford-on-Avon, Warks

Printed and bound in Great Britain by
Clays Ltd, St Ives plc

The paper and board used in this paperback by
Hodder Children's Books are natural recyclable products
made from wood grown in sustainable forests.
The manufacturing processes conform to the environmental
regulations of the country of origin.

Hodder Children's Books
a division of Hodder Headline Ltd
338 Euston Road
London NW1 3BH

1
Magenta

The trouble started last night really. Well, I suppose if you traced it back you could say it started a couple of weeks ago, but I didn't realise that it was trouble at that point. Not *real* trouble. I just assumed it would all peter out. Sadly, it didn't. It was like a snowball, getting bigger and bigger, only I didn't realise quite how big it'd got until last night.

I couldn't quite hear what the phone call was about but, from Dad's pacing up and down the hall, I just knew that it would not be a wise moment to ask for an increase in pocket money. I mean, the Head of Year doesn't usually ring up in the evening for a social chat. The door was slightly ajar and Dad was going backwards and forwards, getting faster and faster, till boy scouts could have used him to start a camp fire. I turned down the volume on the television – just a little. Not so low that he'd realise I was trying to eavesdrop, but just enough to catch the gist.

'No, I haven't seen it . . . Of course . . . I'm sorry . . . I'm sorry . . . Of course not . . . I can only apologise again . . .'

I cringed. Honestly! Didn't he have any self-respect? You'd never catch me grovelling like that to anyone.

'Tomorrow morning, ten o'clock? . . . Yes, we'll see you then.'

Ooops! This was it. It's a miracle the phone didn't break the way he slammed it down.

'Magenta!'

'Yes, Dad?' I put on my most innocent voice.

'Don't play the innocent with me, young lady.'

The next stage was to open my eyes really wide like Sirius does when he wants me to slip him a piece of cheese from the table. Sirius is my dog – as in, Sirius the Dog Star. My dad's an astronomy geek, but actually I thought it was cute too. Anyway, his rolling-eye trick worked on us when we chose him from the dogs' home. The trouble is, when I try it, Dad seems to be immune.

'Where's the letter?' Dad started tapping his foot impatiently.

I knew it was stretching it a bit but I thought I'd give my nun impersonation one more shot. 'Letter? What letter?'

'You know very well what letter. The one telling me that you'd skipped three detentions. The one that was put into your hands by Mrs Delaney personally last week!'

'Oh, *that* letter.' Mrs Delaney is totally round and has a skin condition that causes yellow zits all over her nose. And she always wears pink. Baby pink, salmon pink, strawberry pink, sugar pink – occasionally venturing into the more purply end of the spectrum with a hint of violet. Believe me, it does nothing for her. In fact, it's sometimes difficult to tell where her chin ends and her jumper begins. We call her Mrs Blobby. She is *not* my favourite person and I have a sneaky suspicion that the feeling is entirely mutual.

I tried to stall. 'Err-um, I think it might be in my bag. I put it somewhere safe to give it to you and then when I got home Gran said . . .'

The veins on Dad's forehead were throbbing visibly. 'Don't bring your grandmother into this, Magenta. I have had enough of your excuses. Go and get your school bag.'

'But Dad, I'm . . .' I gave a weak gesture towards the TV in a lame attempt to buy extra time.

'*Now!*' Dad's voice could be surprisingly thunderous at times.

It was a tricky situation and I wasn't quite sure how I was going to get out of it. The first detention had not been justified – all my friends agreed. And the second one was only because I didn't go to the first one, and then the third one was because I hadn't gone to the second. Which, as the original one wasn't justified in the first place, meant that the second and third couldn't possibly be justified either. As I had tried to explain to Mrs Blobby when I got summonsed last week.

It had been a simple mistake. Anyone could've made it. We were in PSE – honestly, what sort of a lesson is that? Personal and Social Education! What they mean is all the tricky bits of growing up that no one really wants to tackle but the government thinks we ought to know. Anyway, we were in PSE and we were discussing the history of childcare. I mean who cares? According to Arlette (who can be a bit of a creep sometimes), Mr Jones was comparing how we were brought up differently from our parents, and the various so-called experts. Perhaps I should have realised that when Mr Jones started talking about Doctor Benjamin Spock, he wasn't leading us in a discussion about the crew of the Starship Enterprise. But, to be perfectly honest, I hadn't really been listening and when I heard the name Spock it was just like a knee-jerk reflex. I'm so used to Daniel next door going on and on about *Deep Space Nine* and *The Next Generation* and *Voyager*, that it just popped out:

'Did you know, Sir, that his ears are made of wax?'

Of course the whole class erupted. And, to be frank, so would anyone with half a sense of humour. But of course I'd forgotten that that excluded Mr Jones. He didn't even have one *grain* of humour in him. Gran would have said Mr Jones 'had a face like a wet weekend and a personality to match'.

'Silence!' he'd bellowed at the whole group and they'd all gone like mice. 'Magenta Orange, stand up. So, you think you're the next best thing to Victoria Wood, do you? Fancy yourself as some sort of stand-up comedienne?'

Now, I knew that this was the sort of rhetorical question teachers like to throw out every now and then. They don't really *want* an answer but if you don't give one they keep pushing and pushing and then accuse you of dumb insolence. Or if you *do* reply they say you're being rude. It was a no-win situation. I looked at Arlette for some sort of support but she just shrugged and gave me a pitying look. I tried Seema, but she just looked away, like she didn't want to know. Seema can be such a coward sometimes. There was nothing else for it, I would just have to do what Dad has spent his life advising me to do: tell the truth.

Big mistake! 'Well, actually Sir, that is one of the

options I'd like to discuss with the careers guidance people.'

I spent the rest of the lesson standing in the corridor. Which, as it turned out, was brilliant, because Adam Jordan, the hottest boy in Year 11 had also been thrown out of his lesson. Talk about credibility! How cool did I look standing against the wall, kicking the radiator in a nonchalant, rebel-without-a-cause type of way? I was sure Adam would be impressed. It wasn't like I was some ordinary wussy little Year 9 kid: I'd been kicked out of a lesson. Adam hadn't *actually* spoken to me, but I suspected he was playing it cool. Not that he needed to: he's so cool, he's almost frozen. He'd casually climbed up the front of some lockers and had been hanging from one of the water pipes that ran along by the ceiling, doing somersaults between his arms. I think he was trying to show off in front of me. Although, later, when I was telling Arlette and Seema, they didn't seem too impressed. In fact they made reference to chimpanzees and orang-utans. Of course I knew they were just jealous. I prefer to think of Adam in terms of an Olympic gymnast.

At the time I was really proud of the way I handled myself. Even when Mr Jones came out, threw a mental and handed me a detention slip, I played it very mature and sophisticated – as soon as he'd gone back in again I tore it up and tossed it in the bin. Well, almost. (This is the bit that I'm not so proud of, although I'm pretty sure Adam was upside down at the time and didn't see what happened next.) The pieces of paper had missed the bin, and, as one of last term's anti-litter campaigners, I really couldn't bring myself to just leave those little pieces of paper all over the floor. So I went to casually walk over and pick them up. Except, I'd been leaning against the wall with my foot against the radiator and my shoe had become wedged in the bars. I tried to wriggle it out elegantly, but that failed. So I gave it an almighty yank. Sure enough my foot was released, but the momentum propelled my leg towards the bin with such force that my shoe flew off. I lurched to try and catch it mid-air but lost my balance and crashed into the bin. Everything spilled out and when the bell went, there I was: scrabbling about on all fours, in a sea of crisp packets and coke cans. Which I could just about have coped with, except that while I was down on my knees I saw *her* coming towards me. She was unmistakable, even at floor level. Anthea Pritchard – year 10's answer to Medusa. Her braided hair tossed casually from side to side as she walked, and her legs seemed to go all the way up to her armpits. Almost everyone stared as she went past – correction, almost every *boy* stared as she went past. The way she wrapped her ankles around each other with every step made me feel quite nauseous. It was as though she thought she was on the catwalk rather than Humanities lower corridor. Although, come to think about it, a catwalk would be the most appropriate place for Anthea Pritchard because she was the biggest cat outside Africa. You could practically hear her snarling as she oozed her way towards the Geography block. I was just watching her and thinking how pathetic all the boys were (honestly, most of them had eyes so far out of their sockets they were more like molluscs than humans), when Adam Jordan dropped down from the water pipe and landed with precision accuracy right by her side.

'Hi, Anth. How ya doing?'

She gave a flick of her braids (Arlette says they're nylon, so it's not like I'm jealous of her hair or anything) and, without even looking at him, she said, 'I'm cool.' I mean, how pretentious is *that*? "I'm cool." Miss Stuck-up Iceberg!

'Ugh!' I squealed at that moment, but not at Anthea – my hand was in something disgusting. Someone had dunked half a tomato sandwich into a tub of chocolate dip and my fingers were covered in a brown sticky mess of soggy bread. To make matters worse, when I'd looked down to see what it was, my hair flopped forward and, without thinking, I pushed it out of the way. So there I was with goo all over my hands and cheek, just at the point that Adam and Anthea walked by. She gave me a look that would have withered most house-plants. I wanted to crawl away and sleep for eternity.

But anyway – I was explaining why Mrs Blobby was phoning my Dad at eight o'clock in the evening and, as you can see, it really was a storm in the proverbial. It certainly didn't warrant a detention and I'd told my form tutor that. He's okay, Mr Kingston; a bit of a get-in-with-the-lads type of teacher, the sort that wears twisted Levis and Nikes and talks about Arsenal all the time, but by and large he's okay. He told me to take it up with Mrs Blobby and that was when I decided to stop following the official line. Mrs Blobby is a no-go area. She teaches Food Technology and she's never forgiven me for mistaking icing sugar for cornflour when we were making cauliflower cheese in Year 7. She's had me earmarked as a troublemaker ever since. Compassion and understanding are two words that are totally alien to her. I'd have had a better chance of survival if I'd decided to leap blindfold from the top of the Millennium Dome.

'Be sure your sins will find you out,' Daniel-next-door said, as though he'd suddenly taken a giant leap forward into the older generation. He's a good bloke really. We're in the same year at school but different tutor groups and we've lived next door to each other for nearly ten years. We went to nursery together, and infant school, and junior school. And when Daniel's mum went back to work, Gran childminded him and his older brother Joe after school. In fact, I suppose Daniel's as near to a best friend as a boy could be. He doesn't mind listening to me going on and on, and he's great when it comes to homework. Our houses are semi-detached and we have rooms that are next to each other. The houses are Edwardian and have these balconies on the front, so in the summer Daniel and I can open our windows, sit on our balconies, turn our music on and talk – it's great. But he can also be a pain, like when he does his 'I told you so' bit. That really pees me off, and he did it about the Mr Jones episode.

'Detentions don't have a sell-by date, you know, Magenta. It's not a case of, "If you don't turn up by the end of October it's expired." Why don't you just do it and get it over with? It's no big deal.'

I tried to explain. 'Well, actually, Daniel, it *is* a big deal. It's a matter of principle. I'm taking a stand on behalf of the repressed minority who are persecuted by teachers. Those megalomaniacs who get their kicks from bullying people who are helpless to defend themselves.'

Daniel wasn't swayed by my opening speech on behalf of the defence and even worse, neither was Dad. He'd gone through my school bag pulling out half a rainforest of screwed up letters – not just the ones about the detentions but others about book fairs and jumble sales and missing homework. I have to admit, even I was amazed at the amount of paper that school wastes!

Well, the long and the short of it is, we're here, sitting outside Mr Crusham's office. I mean, what sort of name is that for any self-respecting headteacher?

Mr Crusham is ancient. Pupils probably still used slates to write on when he started teaching. And he looks like a cross between Father Christmas and Captain Birdseye, but without the smiles – just two beady little eyes peeking out above a beard like an ageing scrubbing brush. He walks about with one hand behind his back, while the other one strokes his beard, pulling it into a point, then suddenly he'll turn and it's like his eyes are boring into you. He gives me the creeps, but parents don't seem to be able to see through him. They seem to think he's the god of education or something.

'Thank you for taking the time to see me,' Dad says as we leave – like The Crusher was doing him a favour! He was no support to me whatsoever. In fact, it was almost as though he was working for the opposition; shaking his head like someone had died and sighing and apologising on my behalf! Every time I opened my mouth to put my side, he put his hand up (you know, like lollipop ladies do to stop the traffic) and said, 'I will discuss this with you later, Magenta' in a really sombre tone.

So now I not only have to do ALL THREE detentions, but I'm also grounded for a month – *and* I have to apologise to Mr Jones and Mrs Blobby.

Hang on a minute – grounded for a month? Let me work that out – *aaaagh*! Oh no! That means I won't be able to go to the Halloween Disco at the youth club and Adam is DJ-ing. *Disaster*! There must be a way round this. I'm sure I can work something out. Now, let me think . . .

2
Daniel

I don't know how I got involved in this. When Magenta says she's had a brain wave it's usually a cue to get out of the way and take cover. Her brain waves are more like tidal waves – sweeping away everything in their path and leaving a trail of destruction in their wake.

'No,' I said (fairly firmly, I thought at the time). 'Leave me out of your little scheme. I don't want any part of it.'

But then she opened those big brown eyes of hers. 'Oh, *pleeeeease*, Daniel. Go on, pleeeeeease. Just for me.'

But I didn't give in – well, not at first anyway. I remained strong. 'No, no, no, no, no! And anyway, you're not even supposed to be round here. You're supposed to be grounded. Your Dad'll kill me if he finds out I've let you in.'

I'd been playing this game on my computer where you go down into the sewers annihilating rats and alligators and spiders and stuff. (And doing pretty well actually – 22,750 points and only one level left

13

before I got to the palace of the mutant King Rat and all his zombie-fied turd-turtles.) I was totally focused; I'd gathered my full quota of methane for making grenades to blow away the turd-turtles and was poised to flush out the King with my demon drain rod, when there was this knocking at my window. I lost concentration for literally a nano-second and before I knew what had happened a giant anaconda had surfaced from the bowels of the sewers (excuse the pun – bowels – sewers – get it?). Well, anyway, this humungous snake had popped up and devoured me and my methane. I was dead! Blown away on a mushroom cloud of sewage and snake guts! I couldn't believe it. It had taken me about an hour to get that far and now I'd have to go back to street level and start from scratch. If it'd been anyone else apart from Magenta I'd have blown *them* away.

'What?' I tried to sound cross, but she was huddled on the balcony between our houses. She had the hood up on her fleece and her hands were tucked up inside the sleeves and she was shivering with her nose pressed up against my French windows.

'Let me in,' she mouthed. She looked so sweet and, well, sort of vulnerable. Now, anyone who knows Magenta knows that 'vulnerable' is the last word you would ever use to describe her but, at ten o'clock on an October night when it was pouring with rain and freezing cold, she did have a certain air of needing protection. So, as much as I was furious with her for disturbing my game, I took pity on her and let her in.

'Daniel, I need you to do me a huge favour . . .'

One day, just perhaps, she might come round and say, 'Daniel, I'd just like the pleasure of your company.' But no, it's always: 'Will you help me with my homework?' Or, 'Will you do such-and-such for me?' Or, 'My computer's crashed, can you fix it?' And this time it was worse! She'd got this nutty idea that I could talk my brother into inviting Adam Jordan round to have a go on his decks. I am so *sick* of hearing about Adam Jordan! It's all she ever talks about – well, no, that's not quite true: she talks about clothes and homework and Robbie Williams too. But most of the time it's Adam-flippin'-Jordan. 'Ooooo-Adam is so lovely.' And, 'Ooooo! You should have seen Adam in the dining room at lunchtime.' And, 'I overheard Adam tell this really funny joke today.' Adam! Adam! Adam! I hate the bloke. And now she's trying to get me to invite him round to my house! The cheek of it! Her stupid, hare-brained idea is that she will just happen to call round and Joe will introduce her to Adam. Adam is then supposed to go all gooey-eyed and wonder why he's never noticed her before. He'll then ask her to help him at the youth club rave and, if she's got the excuse of helping the DJ, her Dad will have to lift his ban and allow her to go.

'Yeah, right! Because life's just like that, Magenta.' I knew I sounded a bit sarcastic but let's look at this logically.

Flaws in the plan:

1) Adam Jordan is so far up his own backside that he's practically inside out and I want no part in trying to set Magenta up with him.

2) My brother Joe will not allow *anyone* near his beloved decks. He's just got them from Dad for his sixteenth birthday and he fancies himself as the next Fat Boy Slim.

3) And, anyway, Joe is unlikely to do anything I say because his idea of brotherly love is not far removed from a piranha's love of human flesh.

4) Magenta's dad is not stupid.

So, how come, you may be wondering, did I find myself in Joe's room about half an hour later, trying to sound enthusiastic about his prize possessions?

'Wow – they really are beauts, aren't they?'

'Don't touch!' He whacked me with a rolled-up

magazine. 'Anyway, what would you know about it? You've only just learned how to press "rewind" on your *Fisher Price* tape machine.' I hoped Magenta realised the humiliation I was going through for her sake. 'So what do you want, anyway?' Joe had his headphones on and was nodding his head like one of those sad little dogs you sometimes see in the back of old people's cars.

I wasn't sure how I was going to word this because Magenta had expressly forbidden me to tell Joe that it was her idea. If I wasn't careful it was going to look as though *I* fancied Adam Jordan!

'I was just thinking, it's the youth club disco coming up in half term.' I wasn't even sure Joe was listening because he had his eyes shut and the whole of the top half of his body was going up and down in a bit of a frenzy, but I went for it anyway. 'And you know Adam's DJ-ing?' I think Joe nodded at this but it was difficult to tell. 'Well, I thought, now you've got your decks, it would be great if the two of you could, somehow, sort of, work out a double act.'

Joe stopped dead and stared at me. I didn't know if he was going to kill me or kiss me.

'That's brilliant!' he said. 'Danny-boy, you are a genius!'

'I know,' I agreed, thinking that I truly was brilliant and should move into politics or the diplomatic service or something with the United Nations.

Then Joe's eyes narrowed – never a good sign. 'So what's in it for you?'

'Nothing,' I said, which was not absolutely true. You see, Magenta had her plan to get introduced to Adam, but I had a second, hidden agenda. Ah, ha – not so dumb after all, am I? You see, I reckoned that, hopefully, when she saw Adam close up she would see what a prat he really was and then she would be eternally grateful to me for:

a) setting up this whole thing

b) showing her the error of her ways

Then I would have a quiet word with her Dad and arrange to take her to the youth club disco and she'd be even more grateful and go out with me and love me forever. Simple!

But of course, I wasn't going to tell Joe all that.

I pretended to be very casual about the whole thing because if Joe got a whiff of what I was up to, he'd do everything he could to mess it up. 'I just thought it would be cool if maybe Adam came round one night, you know, and we could all just hang out . . . and, er, mix a few records . . . and,' (I had over-stretched my knowledge of DJ-ing by this point and

was rapidly running out of things to suggest.) '...
and stuff...'

Joe looked at me for a long time and then grinned.
It was one of those sickening cartoon grins, like Tom
does when he's just about to clobber Jerry with a
frying pan.

'Someone's put you up to it!' he leered.

'Get outta here!' I tried to play it cool and blag it
but, to be honest, blagging has never been my strong
point.

'Now, let me think...' Joe was smirking by
this time. 'Who could possibly gain anything by me
inviting Adam Jordan round here? Oh no, it couldn't
be a certain little next-door-neighbour who's clicked
her fingers and said "Jump, Danny-boy" and my
little bruv's gone, "Of course, Magenta. How high,
Magenta?"'

'Shut up!' I was desperately trying to maintain
some dignity.

'Okay, I'll do it.' I could hardly believe my ears.
There had to be a catch. 'But it'll cost you!' (There it
was.) 'Ten quid.'

'*Ten quid!*' I screeched. I only get a fiver a
week pocket money and the occasional bit extra for
washing Mum's car.

'Take it or leave it, Danno.' Joe can be such a smug

git – I was going to say sometimes but, actually, he's a smug git most of the time. 'Depends how much you want to impress Little Miss Magenta. Or, of course, I could just ask *her* for the money . . .'

'No!' I didn't want Magenta to think I was a total geek. 'No, I'll get you your tenner.' I was going to be washing cars till my hands were as soft as boiled prunes, but if my secret plan worked, it would be worth it.

So, it was all arranged. Adam would come round at about eight o'clock. I'd told Magenta that I'd leave my French windows unlocked so she could come in from the balcony. The idea was that she would just happen to come round to see me about something at about nine – she said she didn't want to look too keen.

She was in and out of my room about a dozen times that evening in different outfits.

'If you're supposed to be just "popping in" to see me, do you really think you'd be dressed like that?' I reasoned. But she didn't seem to like that because she flounced off saying that I was too logical for my own good and didn't I understand the subtleties of being a girl – the easy answer being: No.

Everything was going according to plan – which was good, because this whole enterprise was costing me a small fortune. Adam had brought some records with him – well I suppose he would, when you think about it. He could hardly play CDs on record decks, could he? Anyway he and Joe spent ages setting up Joe's bedroom till it looked like the *Ministry of Sound*. They brought up Mum's wallpapering table for the decks and put her best velvet cushions underneath to act as shock absorbers. There were knobs and turntables, speakers and amplifiers, and leads all over the place so that you could hardly move. Though I hate to admit it, it did look pretty cool in there. Adam said he'd teach me how to mix, which I thought was pretty decent of him, considering my own brother had never offered.

In fact, I was beginning to alter my opinion of Adam. Maybe he wasn't such a jerk. The music was really pounding now and Adam was holding one side of his headphones to one ear while he lined up the other record on the turntable. I'd completely forgotten about Magenta. Adam slid some knobs about while I watched him. It was pretty impressive stuff. In fact, I think Joe was a bit pissed off, because he's obviously not anywhere near as good as Adam.

'Listen,' Adam shouted above the music. 'There are two records playing now. I'll just fade one out and then you can have a go.'

Suddenly, the door to Joe's bedroom burst open. The next ten seconds seemed to last an hour. Joe had been standing behind the door leaning against his chest of drawers. He was trying to look cool, but actually he was sulking because Adam was taking more interest in me than in him. So, when the door opened, the handle hit him square in the kidneys. He screamed and doubled up, accidentally stepping into the speaker on his side of the room and putting his foot through the cone. According to Joe, anyone who knows anything about audio gear will tell you that damaging the cone of a speaker should be punishable by death! So, when he saw what he'd done he was gutted. He turned round and glared at Magenta who was still standing in the doorway, smiling at Adam and totally oblivious to Joe's injury. It looked as though he was going to lurch at her but, before he could, he caught his foot in one of the electric leads that were all over the floor like a cat's cradle and crashed sideways into the wallpapering table.

The table tipped backwards, sending Joe's precious decks into Adam, who was standing behind them. The turntables hit Adam in a very sensitive part of his anatomy, at which point he groaned and folded up like a birthday card. Meanwhile, Adam's very expensive, limited edition vinyl went flying into the air. The next thing I knew, there was a yapping sound from somewhere on the landing and Sirius, Magenta's loony terrier who'd followed her round, shot into the room. He leapt about six feet into the air and caught one of the records in his mouth like a Frisbee (it was quite impressive and I knew Magenta'd been training him for weeks out in the garden, but I didn't really think it was appropriate to clap at that precise moment). Adam let out this pathetic sort of yelp and tried to grab the other record. Unfortunately, what with Joe and Sirius, the cables on the floor had formed a sort of noose and as Adam tried to reach his other record the mesh of cables tightened round his ankles. He toppled into the amplifier, hitting his head and knocking the amp on to the floor. There was a sickening crunch as the amp landed on top of the other record, and then Magenta's voice piped up:

'Hi-ya. It's only me!'

She was wearing the tiniest, stretchiest little skirt I've ever seen outside a box of rubber bands, and seemed completely unaware that the scene resembling Armageddon was down to her.

Joe looked from his speaker to Magenta with a face like a nuclear reactor. I knew he wasn't going to compliment her on her appearance. 'You stupid—'

'Bye, Magenta,' I cut in. 'Not a good time.' I pushed her out of the room, across the landing and back out through my French windows. She put up a bit of a struggle, but, in the interests of damage limitation, I thought it would be best for everyone if she was well out of the way. I locked her on the balcony and, as I went back to Joe's room, I could hear the sound of her banging on the window and shouting, 'Get serious!'

'I *am* serious! Just stay out of the way,' I mouthed back.

My brother was limping about, trying to untangle the knot of cables and salvage some of his equipment. Adam was tussling with Sirius, who still had his teeth into the record and was growling ferociously every time Adam tried to go near him. Then it dawned on me – Magenta hadn't been telling me to 'get serious'. She wanted her dog back.

'Leave!' I shouted. To my utter amazement, Sirius let go of the disc and sat down obediently, with his little tail wagging furiously. He obviously thought this was a brilliant game. I carried him out to Magenta and ushered them both back into their own house.

'Do you think I made an impression?' she asked.

'Oh yes, I think we can safely say you made an impression. But, right now, I think the further away from both Adam and Joe you can get, the better for all concerned. In fact, if you've got any relatives in Tasmania, I would give them a call.'

When I got back, Adam was sitting staring at all the teeth marks and scratches on his record. 'Twenty eight quid that cost me. Twenty eight flipping quid!' he groaned. Then he picked up the pieces of the other record. 'And this one cost twelve. Forty quid's worth of records ruined.' He just kept repeating himself over and over again. 'Forty quid down the drain thanks to that silly cow. What did she want, anyway?'

I shrugged, casually. 'Nothing. She just pops in for a chat sometimes.'

'Oh good,' Adam said, sarcastically. 'I'm glad it was nothing trivial.'

'Don't worry mate,' Joe piped up. 'She'll pay for your records. Daniel will make sure of that, won't you, Bruv?'

'Course. I'll have a word with her tomorrow.'

Right now I'm designing a flyer to advertise my car washing service, and I've also put in for a paper round. So, let me see, ten pounds for the initial deal with Joe, plus forty for the records and Dad thinks he might be able to get the speaker mended for about fifty. That's a round hundred – I should just about pay it off by Christmas! Oh, and I think Mum's present had better be some new velvet cushion covers.

3
Magenta

Could my life get any worse?

Reasons for me to consider emigration:

1) I have had to grovel, like something that's crawled in from the garden, to the horrendous Mrs Blobby and Jones-the-bones. (There is something seriously sinister about that man, but I won't go into it now.)

2) Anyone would think I'd got bubonic plague the way Adam is avoiding me.

3) Even Daniel's barely speaking to me.

4) And as for that lame-brain brother of his ... I could murder him. I was walking down to the dining hall, minding my own business and suddenly this voice booms out along the corridor, 'Red alert! Take cover! Take cover! Demolition woman on the loose!' And everyone started laughing.

Honestly, the way those three are acting, anyone would think it was *me* who smashed up their gear. Personally, I think it's Joe's way of handling his embarrassment. You know, it's one of those bloke things: he can't admit he made a total and utter prat of himself in front of Adam, so he has to blame it on me. You should've seen him the other night when I went round to Daniel's! I mean, sizewise Joe's bedroom is not exactly the Albert Hall, yet he crammed so much equipment in there, you'd think he was auditioning for a gig in Ibiza, not just practising for a youth club disco. I couldn't believe it when I opened the door; it was like walking into a Curry's warehouse. And then he starts falling over and smashing into things and shouting at *me* like its my fault.

In fact, the whole thing was a bit of a washout. The idea was that Adam would see me in a good light and want me to go to the disco with him, but the opportunity just didn't arise.

So, that brings me to my continuing my list of reasons to flee the country:

5) I am no further forward with Adam. In fact, progress has definitely gone into reverse, which means I will have to work even harder now and time is running out. It's less than two weeks to the disco.

And, as if that wasn't bad enough:

6) Gran dragged me off to the dentist yesterday.

This wasn't a total surprise. I went a few weeks

ago and Mrs Munroe (our orthodontist and friendly neighbourhood sadist), pushed half a tonne of peppermint-flavoured mud down my throat. (As if a bit of flavouring is going to make the experience of being choked and gagged any more pleasant – I ask you!) Anyway, I'm not quite sure what happened next. I can only assume that I was in such a state of distress at the time that I was delusional because, apparently, I agreed to this instrument of torture being inserted into my mouth. It is grotesque! When she'd talked about braces, I'd imagined something like Seema has: a dainty little, hardly noticeable, *discreet* retainer than can be taken out on schooldays and other important occasions.

Don't get me wrong – there is no way I want to grow up looking like a try-out for *Bride of Dracula*, but this is obscene! It should be illegal for anyone under the age of twenty-one to be subjected to this type of treatment.

'It looks like the eight forty five from Paddington's going to come hurtling round my gums any minute!' I moaned to Arlette. We were staring into the mirror in the changing rooms of *Up Front*, this really cool clothes shop that's got a coffee bar and everything. Seema had (rather tactlessly, I thought) taken out her brace because she thought she'd seen Hayden West go past and she 'didn't want to look like metal-mouth' if he smiled at her. I wouldn't mind, but she's been going out with Ben Jestico for about six months. *Humph!*

'I'll never be able to open my mouth again,' I wailed.

'Look on the bright side,' Seema piped up. 'If you don't open your mouth, at least you won't get any more detentions from old Jones.'

It was hard to see how my current situation could have a bright side but, actually, Seema was right. My old friend and humourless adversary, Mr Jones, had awarded me yet another detention for yet another miscarriage of justice. Our tutor group has the misfortune to have drawn the short straw on the humanities front. We not only have Bones for PSE, but also for History. Now, don't get me wrong: I have nothing against the Welsh accent. In fact, when I'm listening to an interview with Kelly from the Stereophonics, I go all weak at the knees. But, somehow, it doesn't have quite the same effect when it's Bones wittering on about Neville Chamberlain and Winston Churchill or some other old fossils.

So, anyway, last week, I was sitting at the back of his lesson, planning what I was going to wear to the disco (because I *am* going to go; it doesn't matter what Dad says, it is too important to miss), when suddenly I saw everyone else's hands shoot up. My heart sank. Now, I'm not really into gambling, but I reckoned that out of a class of twenty nine, the chances of him picking me were pretty slim so I put up my hand – just so I'd be less conspicuous.

'Now, let me see ... .' his tinny little sing-song voice went. 'Who hasn't answered a question recently?'

Ooops! That really narrowed it down. In fact, it probably narrowed it down to me and Tariq Anwar and Tariq has only been in the country two weeks and doesn't speak much English. Jonesie was scratching his head as though there was some enormous choice to be made. I tried to slowly sneak my hand down while at the same time writing a note to Arlette: **What was the question?**

She wrote back: **Hitler's name.** Phew – that was easy.

'Magenta?' said Mr Jones. 'Nice to see you participating in the lesson for a change. So, illuminate us.'

I'd show him. 'Hitler,' I said with an air of confidence. The whole class burst out laughing. I glared at Arlette but she tutted and raised her eyes in despair.

31

Mr Jones was revelling in it. 'So, he was Hitler Hitler, was he? A bit like Jerome K Jerome, or Boutros Boutros-Ghali . . .'

'Or Marky Mark, Sir,' piped up Billy O'Dowd, who was out on parole from Mrs Delaney's special withdrawal group.

'Silence!' screamed Bones. It all went horribly quiet. 'I think we'd all gathered that his name was Hitler. I asked for his first name which, had you been paying attention, you would have known.'

'Oh!' I breathed a sigh of relief. Piece of cake! Dad had got *Schindler's List* out on video last year. (I don't know what people did before videos. Imagine all the books they must have had to read.) 'Heil, Sir,' I said with certainty. 'Heil Hitler.'

Well, how was *I* supposed to know? Call me boring but I do have more interesting things to talk to my friends about than the events of a hundred years ago – or whenever Hitler was around.

So that's number seven on my list of reasons to flee the country: another detention. At this rate I might as well just put up a camp bed in Mrs Blobby's office and stay there till half term.

'I can't believe you've had four detentions this term already,' Seema went on as she tried on a gorgeous little pink dress with a slashed hem. (We never buy anything in there; we just try things on.) 'You'd better not get another before the holiday, or your name'll be read out in assembly.' She turned her back to the mirror and looked over her shoulder. 'Does—?'

'*No*, Seema,' Arlette and I both cut in together, 'your bum never looks big in anything.' (A brace she could take out, a long term boyfriend and a tiny bum – life could be so unfair at times.)

But actually, Seema had a point. As part of The Crusher's 'Name and Shame' campaign, anyone who gets five detentions in half a term has their name read out and they have to go and stand on the stage. It's supposed to be humiliating, but actually, it's pretty cool. I mean, all the big names are up there and Adam's been up there twice already since September. Oh, yes! That would be *so* boom!

Anyway, back to our shopping expedition. I had, after a great deal of pleading and eye rolling, persuaded Dad to let me go shopping with Seema and Arlette. It was a Saturday afternoon, so it wasn't like going out in the evening. Therefore, I told him, it was a necessary outing and shouldn't come within the sanctions of 'grounding'. And anyway, I was in desperate need of new trainers – well, ish! The shoes I had my eye on definitely fell into that category.

(Although I didn't think Miss Bignell, our PE teacher would agree.) I'd seen them a few weeks ago in this amazing new shoe shop called *Hide and Sleek*. They had five-inch built-up soles with Velcro fastenings across the front and came in about six different colour ways. I liked the green ones best. They were two-tone with just a very subtle silver trim and would look fantastic with the outfit I was planning to wear for the disco. I'd almost decided on my denim skirt and silver crop top. And, quite honestly, those shoes were made to go with it. But then – crisis! – we saw a very similar pair on a market stall for ten pounds less. They were OK but they just didn't have quite the same, you know, *ooomph*! The soles weren't as high and they didn't have the silvery bit: there just wasn't the same sense of style. So now I had this huge decision to make. Did I get the cheap shoes and have ten quid left over for future investments, or should I go for the ones that I'd had my heart set on? What a dilemma!

'I need to go back and look at the shoes in *Hide and Sleek*,' I said, as we handed the assistant the half dozen outfits we'd been trying on and headed back towards the High Street. 'Which ones do you think?'

'It's up to you,' Seema said. 'Personally, neither of

them are my style. But, hey, it's your money.' I was in a state of turmoil and my two so-called best friends were being no help whatsoever.

And then the strangest thing happened as we were walking along. I saw Arlette elbow Seema in the ribs, like she was trying to prompt her to say something. They both looked a bit sheepish and then Seema said, 'So, is err . . . Daniel going to the disco?'

I stopped dead in my tracks. I wasn't sure what was going on but it looked suspiciously like Seema was trying to suss me out about Daniel. No, she couldn't be. She fancied Hayden West – and she was going out with Ben. She couldn't fancy Daniel *as well* – could she?

'What, Daniel Davis?' I asked.

She nodded. Arlette had wandered away from us and was taking an unhealthy interest in some old men's Y-fronts in the window of a shop that called itself a 'gentleman's outfitters'.

'Yes,' I said, 'Daniel's going. Why?' I looked at her closely, for any giveaway signs.

She shrugged. 'No reason. Just wondered.'

'Do you fancy him?' I asked. I tried not to sound too incredulous but there was no point in beating about the bush.

'No!' she said, a bit too vehemently for my liking.

'You do, don't you?' I squealed. 'You fancy Daniel! Seema fancies Daniel!' I started to sing.

But then she went over to Arlette, who had moved on to a display of string vests, and pulled her away. 'Go on, tell her,' Seema snapped.

Arlette couldn't look me in the eye. 'You *don't*!' I said.

'So?' I've never seen Arlette look so defiant. 'You know what, Magenta? You think just 'cos you live next door to him, you're a world authority on Daniel. And you think that whatever *you* think about him, everyone else should think. But, actually, lots of girls fancy Daniel.'

I was shocked. Daniel! *My* Daniel? He wasn't fanciable material – he was just Daniel. I mean, he's very nice and I do like him but I've never thought of him that way. 'Are you serious?'

'Course,' they both said together.

'How? I mean, why?' I asked, as we walked through town.

'It's his eyes,' Seema said, dreamily.

'What eyes?' I couldn't even have told you what colour they were. I suppose he did have two – I'd have noticed otherwise.

'Oh, they're soooooooo gorgeous,' Arlette chipped in. 'They're that lovely soft hazely-green.'

36

'And his hair.' Seema was looking quite gooey-eyed too for someone who said she didn't fancy him. 'The way it flops forward is so cute.'

Gorgeous? Lovely? Cute? How on Earth could Daniel be described in this way? Had he been mysteriously beamed up to the mother-ship and had a body transplant without my noticing?

'In fact,' Seema went on, 'Arlette wants to know if you'd fix her up with him for the disco?'

Was this some sort of joke, I wondered? Were they winding me up? Well if they were, I'd play them at their own game. And yet they both looked deadly serious. 'Well, I can ask, I suppose – if you're quite sure.'

I was still reeling from the revelation that Daniel might be a sex symbol when we reached *Hide and Sleek*. It was such a bizarre concept that I'd almost forgotten the purpose of our outing.

'Are those the ones?' Arlette was pointing to my shoes. 'They're a bit lairy, don't you think?'

I was just about to take issue with her and her lack of fashion sense when I saw the most amazing sight. I was looking beyond the window display and into the shop itself. There, sitting down trying on some shoes, was Adam Jordan. This was unbelievable. Life was finally smiling on me.

'Quick,' I said to Arlette and Seema. 'Do I look OK?' I gave them a twirl.

'Don't smile too much,' Arlette advised me in view of the engineering works around my mouth area. 'Just play it cool – you know, sort of aloof.'

'Got it. Aloof.' I straightened up and tried to look down my nose in a superior sort of way, which was a bit tricky, because there were some steps down into the sales area. Anyway, I negotiated them without too much hassle. I was ignoring Seema who was, I thought, being a tad negative.

'I don't know why you're bothering. You're already grounded and your dad will go off his trolley when he sees those shoes.'

Aloof. I was going to remain aloof. Adam was trying on these phat trainers at the men's end of the shop but we had to walk past him to the women's section. I decided not to speak to him. I was just going to keep playing it cool and when he noticed me I'd act like I wasn't interested. We strolled down the shop really slowly, you know, like we were queens of the place, until we got to the other end. I asked Seema if she thought Adam had noticed me, but she'd gone. Honestly, trust her. She was off talking to Janet Dibner, the uncoolest person in the entire universe. Janet is such a prize boffin that it could seriously damage a girl's reputation to be seen talking to her. She and Seema are in the top set for English. They seem to get on OK but there was no way I was going to be associated with her – especially in *Hide and Sleek*. To be honest, I was amazed Janet even knew of the place.

So I asked Arlette. 'Has he noticed me?'

She shrugged, 'I don't know. You told me not to look at him.'

'I know, but you could've had a *little* peek.' I was pretending to be looking at the rack of shoes directly in front of us. 'Have a look, have a look,' I whispered. 'Is he looking at me?'

I don't know what came over Arlette at that point and I do sometimes wonder about changing my posse because she turned right round and stared straight at Adam.

'No,' she said, as though she hadn't just made it the most obvious thing in the whole world.

'Have you decided?' Seema swanned back over to us. 'Yuk! What are those things?'

I'd been so intent on Adam that I hadn't realised we were standing in front of a wall full of granny-shoes. (Which would probably explain what Janet Dibner was doing in there.) I hoped Adam hadn't seen me staring at such gross clodhoppers. I looked round quickly and saw the shoes I liked a little further along the rack to my right. It was now a matter of urgency to get away from the pre-war footwear section before Adam saw me and mentally associated me with nubuck moccasins and Jesus-boots. I grabbed Arlette's sleeve and began walking hastily towards the 'under eighty-six' section when, suddenly, it was as though I'd walked straight into an invisible forcefield. There was a noise like Rolf Harris's wobble board and a searing pain shot across my forehead. My nose felt as though it had exploded. I cried out with the pain and felt myself ricochet backwards with such force that I found it difficult to keep my balance. I was still teetering backwards and trying to steady myself when I was aware of a large object behind my knees. I couldn't stay upright any longer and I grabbed for something to hold on to.

As I tumbled, I looked up briefly. Oh, the embarrassment! The humiliation! I saw a reflection of myself with a red weal above my eyebrow and blood beginning to drip from my nose. My mouth was wide open in an expression of horror and, worse still, my Legoland mouthware was on display for all to see! What I'd mistaken for a continuation of shelving to my right had, in fact, been a full-length mirror and I had walked straight into it. I'd then tottered backwards and tripped over an assistant who was kneeling on the floor fitting a pair of shoes to an old dear with a shopping trolley. In a desperate attempt to regain my balance I'd grabbed at the nearest object which, it turns out, was a free-standing rack of shoes that Adam had been perusing and probably the least stable item in the entire store. I went flat on my back and forty thousand left shoes (well, it seemed like that many) came crashing down on top of me. But (this is the most awful part of the whole thing and the biggest reason yet for me to leave the country), they came crashing down on Adam too!

The manager and staff came rushing over. (Which I think was only fair, as they were the ones who put the stupid mirror there in the first place.) But when Adam got up he looked across at me and started to back away.

'No,' he kept muttering as he backed out of the shop. 'Keep her away. Keep her away.'

'Well,' Seema said, trying to console me, 'I think we can safely say he noticed you. But, if I were you, I'd give up this whole "aloof" thing. I don't think you quite manage to carry it off.'

My life is just not worth living!

4
Arlette

It's not fair! My mum and dad have got the completely wrong idea about Magenta. They seem to think she's some sort of she-devil from St Trinian's. And she's not like that *at all*; she just gets a few hare-brained ideas occasionally. The unfortunate thing is, my mum's a history teacher at The Blessed Mother Teresa of Calcutta High School across town and sometimes she sees Mr Jones at meetings and things. It's bad enough for most kids having their parents see their teachers at parents' evenings, but imagine what it's like for me! Mind you, I have to admit, Jonesie does actually like me, so that's not the problem. The problem is he *hates* Magenta. And, from what I can gather, he's not above spreading a bit of manure around the Teachers' Centre either. So the minute Mum and Dad hear anything about her, they go all Gestapo-like. I'm amazed at the hypocrisy of my parents sometimes; they preach about being loving and accepting one minute and then they go and base the whole of their character assassination of poor old Madge on one or two unfortunate incidents – well, three or four, actually. Or maybe five or six. But the ones they hear about are all grossly exaggerated by Old Bonesie. But instead of hearing both sides they'd rather hold her responsible for everything that goes wrong in the world. Take the vegetarian issue for example – poor Magenta got blamed for the whole thing.

'What do you mean, you don't want chicken? You love chicken.' Mum was putting dinner out.

I'd decided ages ago that I wanted to go vegetarian but I'd never had the guts to say so because as far as Mum and Dad are concerned a meal without meat is like a tap without water – except on Fridays, of course, when we have to have fish. (Just in case you hadn't guessed, my parents are heavily into the God-squad. In fact Magenta calls them the 'squadron leaders' – not to their faces, of course.) It took my sister Cassie till she went away to university to pluck up the courage to go veggie. But I didn't want to pollute my body for that long, so Magenta and I made a pact: no food with a face! (We decided that even though potatoes have eyes, they don't count – which was good, because I love chips.)

I looked at Mum, standing there with a fork full of chicken breast, and took a deep breath. 'I'm a vegetarian,' I said.

Dad put down his paper and stared at me like I'd just committed blasphemy. 'Don't go giving your mother backchat, Arlette. It's bad enough your sister's got all these new-age airy-fairy ideas without you jumping on the bandwagon. Eat your chicken.'

Now, Mum and Dad have never resorted to physical punishment or anything like that, but they do have a tendency towards amateur dramatics if Cassie or I do anything they don't approve of. They're masters of the hurt look and the 'you've let us down' routine. In fact, Magenta once said that they ought to write *The Rough Guide To The Guilt Trip*, which I found quite amusing. So, usually, I just go along with what they want. Anything for a quiet life. But this was different. It was something I really cared about.

'No thank you.' I was firm, but authoritative, I thought.

'Arlette,' Dad said, pretty sternly – he's a bit of a softy underneath, but he likes to think of himself as the Jean-Claude van Damme of the software world, 'If the Lord had intended us to be vegetarian, he wouldn't have created animals. Now eat your chicken.' (I really do question his logic sometimes.)

'I'm serious, Dad. I don't want to eat dead animals any more. Magenta and I . . .' As soon as I said it, I knew I shouldn't have mentioned Magenta.

'I might have known that girl . . .' (they never call Magenta by her name, they always refer to her as *that girl*) '. . . would be at the bottom of this somewhere!'

'That girl is not a good influence. I don't want you hanging around with her, you hear!' According to Mr Jones, I'm mixing with the wrong company. It seems he painted Magenta as some kind of urban terrorist, just because she doesn't always listen and gets the wrong end of the stick occasionally – well, maybe a bit more often than occasionally – in fact, most of the time, really. But she's not a bad person.

Anyway, to go back to the veggie issue, I really stood my ground and wouldn't let Mum even put the chicken on my plate in case it contaminated the vegetables. But then we spent the whole meal sitting in silence. When they finally did speak it was only to drone on about eating disorders and to slag off Magenta. Mum's said she doesn't want me going round there any more and Magenta's not allowed to come round to mine. (If she rings up I have to pretend it's Seema.) So when you hear what happened last Thursday, you'll see that I had a bit of a problem.

* * *

Last week had been one of the happiest weeks of my life (until Thursday!). You see, I've had this sort of *thing* about Daniel Davis for ages. I mean really – *ages*: ever since about Year 7. But I never wanted to admit it because Magenta's always going on about him like he somehow belongs to her – I don't mean like a slave or anything, more like a brother. Anyway, I told Seema and she said I should go for it. Which is easy for her to say, she's had masses of boyfriends. But I'd never been out with anyone before and it's OK to fancy him and pretend in my head that he fancied me too, but what happened if he said no? I would've died with embarrassment. I'd never have been able to go to school again. We'd probably have had to move house!

'If you don't ask, you'll never know,' Seema said. (which I didn't find very helpful.) 'You could always ask Magenta to suss out the situation for you.' (Which was a much more sensible suggestion.) So for a couple of weeks I'd been psyching myself up to ask Magenta to ask Daniel out for me, but every time a suitable moment popped up, I bottled it. I thought I would go mad with frustration. In the end, when we were in town last Saturday, Seema jumped in and rescued me. (I'd told a bit of a porky to Mum and Dad because I *forgot* to mention that Magenta would be with us. Luckily I didn't get found out – that time!)

'Honestly, Arlette, you're hopeless sometimes! Just drop it into the conversation, casually.' We'd just come out of *Up Front* and Seema was whispering encouragement to me – or at least she thought it was encouragement. It seemed more like scaring the pants off me from where I was standing.

'Casually! How can I just *casually* happen to mention that I'm passionately in love with her next-door-neighbour?'

'Watch and learn, girl,' she said, sidling up to Magenta.

But I couldn't. I couldn't stay there and risk the humiliation. I'm sure Magenta thinks I'm a bit pervy or something, because I was so embarrassed when Seema was talking to her, I ended up staring into this old men's shop at all the long johns and other gross stuff that looks as though it's been made out of dishcloths. But joy of joys, Magenta agreed! She said she'd set it up. I thought she seemed a bit funny about it, but maybe that was my imagination.

I cannot tell you how nervous I was that night. At one point I thought I was going to throw up. I couldn't eat. I couldn't sleep. I got myself into a right state. Then, we'd just got back from church on Sunday when the phone rang.

'I'll get it!' I screamed, knocking Dad out of the way to grab the phone before either of them could answer it and recognise Magenta's voice. 'Hi, Mmm . . . Seema!' It was amazing how easily I could lie when I had to. 'Well? Any news?' I had to be subtle just in case Mum or Dad was listening.

'He said OK.'

'He didn't!' I couldn't believe it.

'Yes, he did. I've just told you he did!' I thought Magenta's voice sounded a bit tetchy but I was so happy I didn't care.

'Oh, wow! Oh, that is so . . . Oh, I can hardly . . .' I was sooooooo excited.

'So anyway,' Magenta cut in, 'do you fancy coming with me on Monday after school to buy those shoes?'

I didn't actually want to talk about shoes, I wanted to carry on talking about Daniel but it didn't matter anyway because Dad came through to the hall and called me for lunch. I spent the rest of the day as though I was bouncing on clouds.

Daniel met me off my bus on Monday morning and it's just been great ever since – well, most of the time. Sometimes it's been a bit awkward though. Like, now that we're officially an item, Daniel walks me to the bus stop and waits with me till my bus comes. But, because Daniel always used to walk home with Magenta, she comes with us. It's already beginning to feel like there's three of us in this relationship. It doesn't look as though Daniel objects though. In fact, the other day he insisted we wait for Magenta after she'd done her detention. Not that I minded really – it meant we could stand at the gates together for an hour after everyone else had gone, which was really great. He's so sweet.

Anyway, to get back to Thursday. It was the last day before half term. (I love it when the teachers have a training day on the Friday – it means we get an extra day added on to our holiday. It also means I get a day at home on my own while Mum still has to go to work!) Anyway, we were at the bus stop getting into the holiday spirit, (the three of us!) when Magenta started tugging my arm.

'Look, look!' she whispered. 'It's Adam Jordan. It's him.'

To be honest I don't know what she sees in him – if they gave out Oscars for vanity, Adam Jordan would be up there with *Star Wars*! 'I know,' I said, thinking how dreamy Daniel looked compared to Adam and how lucky I was. 'He sometimes gets the same bus as me.'

Then Adam went up to Daniel and they did this boy thing of punching their fists together. I've never understood why they do that; it looks like they're doing 'one potato, two potato' like we used to do in primary school to pick teams. But they seem to think it looks all butch and macho.

'How ya doin', Danno, my man?' Adam said. (Talk about pretentious!)

And then Daniel, who has never, to my knowledge, tried to play the hard-man, started acting all strange. 'I'm good,' he said, putting on this odd expression and nodding his head. Then he started to squirm and make this strange squeaky sort of sound and I noticed that Magenta had got her finger embedded in his ribs and was prodding him furiously. 'You remember Magenta, don't you?' Daniel said to Adam.

At which point Adam did a double take and seemed to take a couple of steps back. 'Yeah, yeah,' he said, a bit hastily. 'Once met, never forgotten – or in your case, twice met, etched on my memory with indelible ink.' Then he moved off to the front of the queue.

Now, my interpretation of this exchange suggested that Adam wanted to be as far away from Magenta as possible, but somehow she got the completely opposite message. 'Wow! Did you hear that? He remembers me!'

'Well, that's probably because on both occasions

that he's met you, he's been practically maimed for life,' I pointed out.

But I'll give Magenta credit for one thing: she doesn't give up easily. 'There's no such thing as bad publicity,' she says. 'It's just a bit of a false start. Anyway' – here came the crunch – 'I've had a brainwave!'

Daniel started to shake his head. 'Oh no. I'm outta here. I want no part in it – whatever it is.'

'Chill,' she said. 'You don't need to have any part in it – except to tell Gran I'm doing my homework at Arlette's tonight and I'll ring Dad later for a lift home. OK?'

Now, I've already told you that my parents are not exactly Magenta's number one fans so I was a bit worried about how I was going to get around this. I tried to make a joke of it, but I don't think it was a very effective one. 'Err – *hello*! Are you going to ask *me* if you can eat at my house? And what about my mum – doesn't she get a say in this?'

'I like your mum. She'll be cool – don't worry about it.'

And the next thing I knew she'd sent Daniel off home. And he went! I mean, I'm supposed to be his girlfriend, right? But did I get a say in it? I didn't even get a goodbye kiss. He just went off and left me standing at the bus stop with Magenta, who couldn't even look at me when she was talking to me because she was craning so hard to see Adam that her neck was rapidly taking on the appearance of a giraffe's. I was a bit miffed to say the least.

'Okay, so I fixed you up with Daniel, right?' Magenta was saying to a point somewhere above my head, and my heart sank. I had the distinct impression that this was going to be payback time. 'So, I'm thinking, wouldn't it be brilliant if we *both* had dates for the rave next week.'

'Well, it would,' I agreed, 'but there are two problems here, Magenta. One is that you're meant to be grounded.'

'A minor detail,' she said. 'Dad'll come round – trust me. So what's number two?'

Now, don't get me wrong. Magenta is my best friend. I haven't known her as long as Seema has; they were at primary school together. But we all started in Year 7 and have been a posse ever since. One of the things I like about her is the way she just goes for things. The downside of course, is that she doesn't always think things through. It's usually a case of 'act first, engage brain later' with Magenta. Trust her? I'd rather trust a tree surgeon to take out a splinter.

'Number two,' I went on, 'is that you fancy Adam and there's no way I can fix you up with him.' Then I had my own brainwave. 'But Daniel says Sam Pudmore's got a bit of a crush on you. I could see what I could do in that direction.'

'What, Spud? You have *got* to be joking!' Granted her reaction was a little less enthusiastic than I'd hoped, but then she seemed to warm to the idea. 'Has he really got a crush on me? Wow!' Unfortunately, she then reverted to her initial shock, horror response. 'How could you even think of it, Arlette? His ears look as though they belong on the plains of Africa and he's got that gross br... Well, it's not his brace that's gross...' (I think she stopped when she remembered that she was not entirely free from structural engineering in the mouth region herself) 'it's all those elastic bands all over it. He looks like an explosion in a rubber factory!'

'He's not so bad,' I tried to reason. And actually, it was true; Spud was an OK guy. Unfortunately his brace was one of the worst I think I've ever seen, but his ears weren't that big and his hair was long enough to cover them anyway. 'I think he's quite sweet.'

Magenta gave me one of her looks. 'I'm not even going to go there, Arlette. My sights are set on bigger fish and this is how we're going to go about it.'

Her plan was very simple really – simple in the respect that it had to have been thought up by someone who was, herself, simple.

Step one:

. . . was to follow Adam as far as he went on the bus. Usually I get off before him, so I'd no idea if he got off at the stop after me or went right on to the terminus, in which case, we'd be lucky to get home before midnight and we'd both be grounded.

'Don't worry, if that happens I'll think of something,' Magenta reassured me. 'Anyway, he wouldn't be at our school if he lived that far away, would he?' This was true and, I have to say, surprisingly logical for Magenta. And I have to admit that, as we embarked on our surveillance mission, I did feel a teeny bit excited. That's another thing I really like about Magenta – life's never dull when I'm with her.

Adam went to sit upstairs, so Magenta said it would be less obvious if we stayed downstairs. That way we could watch every stop and if he came down we could leap off at the last minute so that he wouldn't suspect he was being followed.

'Magenta,' I whispered, as the bus sailed past the stop where I would normally get off, 'doesn't this count as stalking or something? Can't we get done for a criminal offence?'

But before she could answer, Adam and a crowd of boys came running down the stairs. Magenta practically threw herself forwards pretending to be looking for something in her bag. 'I don't want him to see me,' she whispered, which seemed a bit strange as I thought that was the object of the whole exercise!

It didn't matter about me being seen, though, because I'm on that bus anyway, so I watched what Adam did as he ran off the bus. There was an old woman sitting near the bottom of the stairs wearing a big blue hat. As Adam ran past her he flicked his hand under the brim and knocked it off and all his mates laughed. I picked it up as Magenta and I made a dash for the door.

'Did you see what he did?' I said, hoping she might come to her senses about Adam. 'He knocked that woman's hat off.'

'Well, it would've been an accident,' she said. 'He probably didn't even realise he'd done it. Come on, we're losing them.'

Step two;

. . . was to follow Adam to where he lived. And actually following the boys was surprisingly easy.

They were so engrossed in their conversation that they didn't seem to notice us and if they did stop, we simply ducked into doorways or behind a tree.

We followed them on to the Orchard Estate. It's this fairly modern estate of flats and houses with lots of greenery and trees (so masses of hiding places!). Eventually the group started to drift off in different directions. Adam was one of the first to break away. We were trailing him (at a discreet distance of course), over the road and then across this massive grass verge to a little parade of shops. He stopped at the sweet shop, so we stayed outside and made out we were chatting behind one of the trees on the grassy bank. When he came out we saw him turn down the narrow alley next to the shop. And then suddenly, he'd gone! Vanished! Disappeared into thin air!

Honestly, it could've only taken us a couple of seconds to get into the alley but there was no sign of him. It was a bit creepy down there, I thought. There was a narrow path that ran behind the backs of two rows of houses with high fences and it smelled. It must have been bin-day the next day because there were dustbins everywhere. 'Never mind,' I said. 'Maybe we can follow him another day and find out where he lives.'

Anyone would think I'd sworn at her, the way Magenta looked at me. 'No way! I'm not giving up now. Come on.'

Now, when I said the fences were high, I meant they were higher than shoulder height – but unfortunately not higher than our heads. Which meant that to go along the alley without being seen we had to crouch down a bit – talk about a killer on the knees! Each fence had a gate in it that led into a small garden and most of the houses had lights on, so that we could see through the fence and into the kitchens. We went the whole length of the alley and back, without seeing Adam in any of the houses. It was starting to get dark and I was a bit worried because I hadn't let Mum know that I'd be late – or that I'd be bringing Magenta home with me. I was also getting very cold.

'Come on, let's call it a day. I'm freezing.' I was also getting a bit bored. I mean, it wasn't like we were stalking Leonardo DiCaprio or anything. This was Adam Jordan, for heaven's sake.

'Ssssh! Wait!' Magenta whispered. Just then an upstairs light went on in the very first house in the alley – the one we were right outside! No wonder we'd lost him; while we were trying to surreptitiously hide behind one of the trees outside the sweet shop, he'd slipped into the first gateway! So all the time we were crawling up and down the alley getting cramp in our legs and frostbite in our fingers, he was nice and warm in his house. Grrrrr! 'Oh, look at him. Isn't he dreamy?' Magenta dribbled, going all gooey-eyed.

Adam was standing looking out of the window with his arms folded. I wanted to say: *Actually, Magenta, no I don't think he is that dreamy. In fact, he might be good looking, but he certainly knows it and personality wise, I think he definitely borders on the nightmare-ish side.* But I didn't quite have the heart to disillusion her. At this point we were supposed to put step three of the plan into action; just hang around looking cool until he noticed us – or at least, noticed Magenta so that she could undo some of the damage to her reputation.

'I thought you said look cool, not *drool*,' I said, after we'd been crouched down outside his fence for approximately half a lifetime. It was certainly beginning to look like another of Magenta's loopy ideas. I don't think either of us had counted on him going straight indoors or on us having to crawl up and down the alley. I just wanted to go home. Just then we heard shouting from Adam's house. We couldn't make out what was being said, but he started throwing his arms about and seemed quite angry. Then he disappeared from the upstairs window. The next thing I knew Magenta was pushing me backwards.

'Go, go,' she was shouting in a whispery sort of way. 'He's coming out. He mustn't see us.' She was edging her way backwards, flapping her hands indicating for me to go back out of the alley. The trouble is, we'd both forgotten about the dustbins. And the sweet shop on the corner had two of those huge metal things on wheels just sitting in the middle of the alley right behind us. The next thing I knew, I'd backed into one of them. Then Magenta backed into me and we both tripped backwards and ricocheted off the big bin and into one of the smaller dustbins. It rolled over and I felt myself teetering for a split second before Magenta crashed into me and we both tumbled over the bin and down the grass verge. Meanwhile, the first big bin had rolled into the second big bin and they were gathering momentum. There was quite a slope down past the side of the sweet shop but when they reached the grass verge their wheels jammed and both bins tipped up, spilling their contents everywhere just as we landed in the road outside the sweet shop.

'What a mess! My mum's going to kill me!' I

shouted, but then I looked up. She wasn't going to get a chance. This monstrous great motorbike was hurtling towards us. There was a screech of brakes and a blast of a horn from a car coming the other way. We were well and truly stuffed and it was all because of Magenta drooling over some over-inflated dongo-head.

'Help!' She shouted and buried her face in my blazer. 'Save me, Arl! Save me!'

I wrapped my arms round her to protect her, closed my eyes and waited for the inevitable . . .

5
Magenta

Things are so looking up in my life! I can't wait to tell you what's happened. But I'm getting ahead of myself. Let me take you over the last week.

It was last Saturday and I'd gone round to Daniel's.

'What *has* happened to your face? Are you okay?'

I have to say, I was quite touched that he seemed so concerned about my minor mishap in *Hide and Sleek*, but that wasn't why I'd gone round there. 'It's nothing,' I said, sounding extremely brave I thought.

'It doesn't look like nothing. It looks like you've done a few rounds with Lennox Lewis.'

I think he must have been referring to some boxer or other, but I'm anti-blood sports, so I just ignored him. 'Really, I'm fine. Now look . . .' I sat down on the edge of his bed and studied him while he twiddled with his joystick. The reason I'd gone round there was to ask him if he'd go out with Arlette. I have to say I was a bit shocked when I found out that she fancied him. I had to take a serious look at him for myself – not *for* myself you understand, because obviously Adam is the only boy for me, but to have a look at Daniel – objectively. He was quite nice-looking, I suppose, although I'd never really thought of him in that light before. It was hard to think of him as heart-throb material but both Arlette and Seema had said they fancied him – not that Seema counts because she's been going out with Ben since she was born practically – well, the summer, anyway. It didn't seem right somehow to be sitting there eyeing up Daniel but I suppose there was a certain something about him that made him quite endearing – in a strictly platonic sort of way, of course. 'Daniel,' I got back on to the subject. 'What do you think of Arlette?'

I have to say he didn't seem that impressed. 'She's OK, I suppose. Why?'

'Do you fancy her?'

He shrugged. 'Dunno. Never thought about it really.' And then this very odd look came on his face. It was the sort of look people get when they're hatching a cunning plan. 'Why? Does she fancy me?'

Honestly, the arrogance of boys! Don't ask me why, but I felt a bit annoyed with him. 'Well, yes, actually, she does, and she wants to know if you'll go out with her.'

'OK,' he said – just like that. He didn't have to even think about it – OK! And then he grinned at me like he was really made-up with himself.

'Are you sure?' I asked. 'I mean, don't feel obliged if you don't want to.'

'No, I'm cool. That'll be great.' Then he went on playing on his computer like I wasn't there and smiling to himself.

'OK then, I'll ring her and tell her, shall I?'

'Excellent.' He was grinning like some drunken Cheshire Cat and making all these very juvenile noises to accompany his computer game, so I left him to it.

Dad was in a foul mood. He was stomping around the house shouting at me and Gran and even poor little Sirius. Now I could understand how he might be mad at me because I think he got a whiff of the fact that I'd got another detention from old Bonesie, although I don't know how – unless Mrs Blobby's been writing to him behind my back, or someone's squealed on me. Anyway, he'd been going on at length about the perils of being a delinquent and ending up on the streets living in a cardboard box with no GCSEs. (Not that I think qualifications would be the top of my worry list if I was living rough, but parents have bizarre logic at times.) And Gran had peed him off because she'd been serving up what Dad calls 'cartoon fodder' all week. To be fair to Gran, pizza is my all-time favourite food so she could have been doing it out of compassion for me because, let's face it, nothing else in my life was going well at that point and a girl has to have some comforts.

'Mother!' You can always tell when Dad's mad at Gran because he calls her *Mother* rather than *Mum*. 'Is there a *reason* why this is the fourth pizza we've had this week?'

'I thought you liked pizza.'

'I do. I also like Christmas, but I wouldn't want it every day.'

'Well, it may surprise you to know, Curtis, that I have a life of my own. I am not just chief cook and bottle washer for you and Magenta and if you don't like the meals I prepare, I suggest you start to do some of your own shopping and cooking sometimes.' (Have you noticed how adults always talk very formally when they're mad at each other?)

So we had our pizza in silence and then Dad went off on one about the state of the house (with particular focus on my bedroom) and the appalling standard of Saturday night television. In fact he was generally in a bigger strop than Stroppy Stropperson about everything – and it carried on all over the weekend. I was pleased to get back to school on Monday.

But the downside of going back to school of course was that I had to put up with 'the young lovers' smooching all over the place. At break, at lunchtime, on the way home, Daniel and Arlette were all over each other – ugh! Some people have no sense of decorum. I even came out of my detention on Tuesday to find them still snogging at the front gate – at half past four! And I had Arlette going on and on and on about how they were going to go to the cinema and how Daniel was going to take her to the disco in half term and how he'd asked her to go over to his during the holiday. And then Daniel's going on and on and on about how gorgeous Arlette is and what a good kisser she is (a little bit more than I need to know, I think) – yawn, yawn, yawn! People in love can be so boring. I'd never be like that. When Adam and I start going out (and it is *when* and not *if*), I'm going to be very laid-back about it. I won't bore the pants off everyone.

Anyway, last week was generally a bit of a write-off. Apart from anything else, I'd hardly seen Adam. I had hoped that if I got another detention and had to stand on-stage he might notice me. I'm convinced that he just needs to see me in the right light and he'll like me. But I couldn't even manage that last week, although I did try.

At the beginning of netball I went up to Ms Bignell, our PE teacher and made my protest. Quite why she went into teaching with a name like that, I'll never know. She must have known what she'd get called and the irony is, she's tiny. She's got a physique like a flower fairy. But to be frank, she can't control the class and dishes out detentions like Smarties. So I reckoned I was on a pretty sure thing with Big Nell.

'Hurry up and get changed, Magenta.' She poked her head out of her little office. I'd love to know what goes on in those PE teachers' offices. Are they secret gambling dens? Or are they like the Tardis and really go on for miles?

'I'm not going to do it, Miss,' I said – not too defiantly, because I sort of feel sorry for Big Nell. Apparently last year's Year 11s locked her in the equipment cupboard and no one missed her for four hours. It was only when the caretaker was doing his rounds that he heard her crying and let her out. She'd missed two lessons and a hockey practice and no one said anything about her not being there. So I decided to be gentle with her – I only wanted a detention.

'Why? Are you injured?' She was like a little

mouse with her nervously twitching nose and squeaky voice.

'No – well, at least, not yet, but I've read this article and it says that the constant pounding of young girls' knees and ankles on asphalt is damaging. It leads to arthritis and all sorts of terrible things and says that we could all end up in wheel-chairs if we do it, so I'm sorry, Miss, but I'm not going to do netball any more.' I was quite pleased with the way I acquitted myself and was braced to look shocked when she issued my detention – I was even going to protest a little (not too much, you understand, in case she rescinded it). But then it all started to go pear-shaped because Miss Crumm, the head of department, came to the door. Now she *is* a big woman. She's built like a rhinoceros, with a face to match!

'What's this?' said The Rhino. 'Magenta's revolting?'

(Ho, ho, ho, send for a sewing machine, I've split my sides! Honestly – you'd think that if she was going to become a comedian she'd get some new material.)

'No, Miss. Well . . .'

'Don't bother with your little speech again, Magenta, it was pathetic enough the first time round. Utter tosh and nonsense! I've been playing netball for years and look at me – fit as a flea!' For a split second I quite liked poor old Big Nell because I caught her eye and she looked as though she was trying desperately not to laugh. I must have given her a conspiratorial smile in return because the next thing I knew Miss Crumm was booming at me, 'So, you think it's amusing, do you?'

'No, Miss.'

'Well, we'll see how funny you find this. In order to save the knees of you and all your friends, the whole class can spend this lesson running round the perimeter of the playing field. Nice soft grass to protect your joints, eh, Magenta?'

There was this chorus of 'Aw, Miss! That's not fair!'

Sophie Parker, this massive girl who plays goal defence for the county under-18s was not happy. 'Cheers, Magenta – nice one!'

'You'll be grateful one day.' I tried to bluff it out.

Then I could hardly believe my ears because Arlette started to give away my whole plan to the entire form. 'She doesn't really want us to stop playing netball. It's just that she fancies Adam Jordan and she thinks that if she can get another detention this half term she'll be called up on to the stage and he'll be impressed . . .' she was explaining to Candy, whose auntie plays centre for the Jamaican national squad.

'So that's your little game, is it?' Miss Bigears Crumm bellowed. 'Well I'm going to nip this little Orange Revolution in the bud. I think the rest of the staff will be extremely interested to hear your scheme. I shall put up a notice in the staffroom immediately advising everyone who teaches you to avoid giving you detentions but to find a punishment which fits the crime. Let's see how *that* improves your love life. Now, over to you, Ms Bignell, and any more dissent from our rebel here, just let me know. I'm sure I can find something appropriate to keep her occupied.'

Even Ms Lovell, my art teacher, had a go at me about it. Ms Lovell's great. She really likes me – mainly because I'm so good at art. Or at least, she *used* to like me.

'I read a rather disturbing note about you on the staffroom notice-board, Magenta.' She came over as I was putting the final coil on this clay pot I'd been making.

'Oh, that's just old Miss Crumm getting her thermals in a knot,' I said, dismissively.

She nodded in a sort of sad way so that I thought I'd done something incredibly stupid. I really like

Belinda – Ms Lovell says we can call her Belinda in the art room so long as we don't call her by her first name to other members of staff – she's really cool. She's not your usual funky art teacher. She's not even really trendy or anything. In fact, she's a bit of an earth mother type – probably knits her own knickers out of organic oatmeal and that sort of thing, but I really like her. We try to get her to tell us about her boyfriend, but she won't ever say anything. I hope she's got one. Sometimes we imagine what he'd be like. So far we've decided that he's got long hair tied back in a ponytail and he wears rainbow-striped jumpers – hand-knitted of course. He'd be called 'Seth' or 'Cobb' or something manly, but we can't think what sort of job he'd do. Probably something like an Eco-warrior, fighting for the freedom of the rainforests. Whenever we ask her if we're right, she just smiles. She's great. It was Belinda who got me into being veggie.

So I was really choked when she said, 'You know, Magenta, you have many wonderful qualities and attributes, you don't need to try to impress people by being a rebel. And if you do, then maybe they're not worth impressing.'

I was gutted. It kept niggling me all lesson. But then, I thought, she's getting on a bit so she's probably forgotten what it's like being my age. I mean she's not as old as Dad or anything, but she must be at least twenty six or seven. So I just tried to put it to one side. It completely ruined my art lesson though. And as if that wasn't bad enough I had to spend lunchtime with the two pairs of star-crossed lovers: Seema and Ben, and Arlette and Daniel. It was like trying to eat in a slush factory! Talk about being put off your food!

But things started to take a turn for the better on Thursday. I was walking to the bus stop with Arlette and Daniel – he walks her to the bus every single night after school since they've been going out. I mean, it's not like they don't see enough of each other during the day or that she doesn't know the way or anything. But anyway, there we all were at the bus stop, when Adam Jordan comes along.

'Oh, he often gets my bus,' says Arlette. I couldn't believe it! Why has she never mentioned this vital fact before?

Well, it seemed like the answer to all my prayers. I think the reason I haven't made much progress with him is that he hasn't really seen me at my best so far and I think he may have got the wrong impression of me. So I've been trying to get him to notice me – in a cool way – and then when I saw him at the bus stop I had this brilliant idea. I sent Daniel off with a message to Gran that I was going to Arlette's for dinner so we could follow him and find out where he lives. Then we could just sort of hang around looking cool and maybe he'd start chatting to us. And then, who knows what could come of it? I have to say, Arlette didn't seem too keen on the idea. I don't know what it is with her – she always seems to have a downer on Adam. Maybe she secretly fancies him and doesn't want me to get off with him so tries to put me off? She even tried to pair me up with Spud. I mean, Spud's *OK*, but on the cool factor gauge he doesn't even register. And if I thought *my* brace was bad, it's nothing compared to Spud's. I feel quite sorry for him really. Although, secretly, I was quite chuffed when she said he fancied me. I mean, it's always nice for a girl to hear that she's got admirers.

So, anyway, we started to follow Adam. I had to keep my head down on the bus – I didn't want him to see me and get the wrong idea. I mean, it would be so easy to misinterpret it and think that I was some sort of sad dweeb! There was a bit of a problem though because instead of hanging with his mates, like any normal boy would've done, he went straight home! Thanks to my expert detective skills however, we managed to suss out his house but, by that time, Arlette had started moaning about being cold and wanting to go home. Honestly, I do wonder about her sometimes; she's got no stamina. And then, just at the moment he came out of the house and we were supposed to move into cool-pose, disaster struck.

I'd signalled to Arlette to move back away from the house so that it didn't look as though we were on a stake-out or something, but she only went and crashed into a dustbin! One of those huge industrial jobs on wheels! It started to roll down the footpath crashing into this other bin on its way, but I couldn't stop it because I was already backing away from Adam's house and as I reversed into Arlette we both fell sideways into this ordinary little domestic dustbin! What a catastrophe! Before I knew what was happening we were both rolling down the grass verge covered in bits of soggy cornflakes and stale bread with these two commercial bins rumbling after us like demented Daleks. Then the big bins just sort of keeled over and everything poured out on to the grass verge. It was gross.

We ended up in the middle of the road and I was desperate to get out of the way before Adam appeared and saw me in yet another unfortunate situation. But just as I was about to get up, Arlette grabbed hold of me and started screaming at the top of her voice.

'Aaaagh! Help, Magenta! Help!'

At first I thought she was being a bit over dramatic – I mean, it was just a bit of smelly leftovers, nothing a bath and a trip to the dry-cleaners wouldn't put right. But then I looked up. A huge great motorbike was heading straight for us. Arlette was a gibbering wreck so I put my arms around her to protect her; she was obviously scared stiff. And then the bike veered off across the other side of the road, missing us. Phew! I thought, but then I saw that it'd driven straight into the path of a car, which swerved towards us. What a nightmare! Arlette was sobbing by now, so I had to hold her very tight to reassure her. As I looked up, the car skidded by us, mounted the kerb and ploughed up the grass verge.

'You stupid idiots!' The man had got out of the car and didn't seem too happy, although why he was taking it out on us, I don't know – it was the motorbike rider he should've been shouting at. Just then these two people in black leathers came striding over like a pair of Darth Vaders or something. I was just about to ask them if they were aware of the speed limit when out of the corner of my eye I saw Adam Jordan sidling off in the opposite direction, shaking his head. Life is *so* unfair at times! Why is it that he always seems to be around when things are going wrong?

Just then the smaller Darth Vader took off this enormous black helmet.

'Uh-oh,' snivelled Arlette.

'Magenta? Arlette? What on Earth . . . ?'

'You mean you actually *know* these two imbeciles?' shrieked the man from the car. 'Do you realise we could all have been killed . . . ?' He was going on and on, but I wasn't taking a great deal of notice to be honest. I was looking across the road to where the motorbike was propped up on its stand.

Maybe life *wasn't* so unfair. After all, as Gran and Auntie Venice are forever telling me when we play *Newmarket* at Christmas, it's not so much the cards you're dealt, but how you play them that counts. And life had just dealt me a hand that was going to add a very interesting twist indeed.

6
Magenta

I knew everything would turn out all right. Didn't I tell Arlette to stop worrying and trust me?

Mind you, I didn't know that the *reason* it would turn out all right was because my grandmother is a secret Hell's Angel. I don't know what's going on with her at the moment; whether she's going through some late-life crisis or what. It turns out she and Auntie Venice have a motorbike stashed at Auntie Vee's and they go out for illicit spins on their days off. But, whatever they're up to, it turned out great for me because Gran knows that I know that if Dad ever found out about her and Auntie Venice being The Kawasaki-kids, he would go into orbit faster than you can say 'Starship Enterprise'. I thought it was bad enough last year when she came back from the hairdresser's looking like an entrant in a Tina Turner look-alike competition who'd been accidentally plugged into the National Grid. The New Year fireworks looked like a soggy sparkler by comparison – so can you imagine what effect this would have, with the mood he's been in recently?

So it was pretty straightforward really. Gran and I did a deal: I agreed not to tell Dad about her mean machine if she would persuade him to let me go to the youth club rave. And my wonderful Fairy Grandmother came up with the goods – she knew it was in her own interest. She talked Dad round, so Magenta-ella is going to go to the ball after all.

Arlette got all prissy when I told her. 'I think you're despicable!'

I made a mental note to look up the word *despicable* as soon as I got off the phone but I could tell from the tone of her voice that it wasn't a compliment. 'Why?' I tried to sound suitably hurt.

'Because you're blackmailing your own grandmother!'

I was shocked. I mean, blackmail is a pretty ugly word. 'No, I'm not. I'm just using the situation to my best advantage,' I reasoned. After all, who's Arlette to get so self-righteous all of a sudden? I mean, it's not like *she's* been exactly honest with *her* parents – as I found out last Thursday night, when Daniel came hammering on my French window like the Spanish Inquisition.

'OK, so Arlette says you're going to explain to me why I have to pretend she was at my house until about five o'clock tonight!'

I mean, who did he think he was, standing on my balcony with his hands on his hips trying to look all butch and heavy? Arnold Schwarzenegger? Puleeeease! Just because he's got a girlfriend he thinks he's so cool.

'Daniel!' I was a bit annoyed because I'd smudged my nails opening the window for him. 'You can't just come barging in here whenever you want, you know.'

'Why not? You do it to me,' he said, which is *so* not true. 'Anyway, I want to know what sort of trouble you've got Arlette into.'

'Me?' I said, desperately trying to think of something that wouldn't make it sound like I was some sad Adam Jordan groupie. 'That is *so* unfair, Daniel. Why do you automatically assume it's down to *me*?' I sat down on my bed feeling upset if I'm honest – I mean, I bet he didn't ask Arlette what sort of trouble *she'd* got *me* into, did he?

'Well, I look at it this way: first you get one of your hare-brained ideas, then you go off with Arlette and then Arlette rings me and asks me to lie to her parents . . .'

'Not lie, exactly,' I interrupted. 'More – support her.'

'Oh I see, I'm supporting her, am I?'

'Of course.'

'Oh, so let's see, what is the truth of the situation? Was Arlette at my house until five o'clock? I don't think so! But if I tell her parents that she was, I'm not lying, I'm *supporting* her?'

'Exactly!' Phew! He seemed to have got it at last – Daniel can be a bit slow sometimes.

'Supporting her by lying!' he shouted and then he stomped off back to his own room. Honestly, talk about a drama queen. What *is* his problem? I mean, it's not like it was some huge, rot-in-hell-for-all-eternity type lie. It's only a teensy little one. And if Arlette's parents didn't have her down as odds on favourite for the first female Pope, she'd be able to lead a normal social life and not have to tell porkies about innocent little escapades. It's their own fault really.

But anyway, all that happened last week so it's ancient history now. Tonight's the night and all I have to worry about now (*all* I have to worry about? It's been occupying my mind for most of half term actually) is my ball gown. So – which outfit shall I wear? I had planned to wear the silver top and a denim skirt with the green shoes but I'm not sure it's dramatic enough and I want to make a real entrance tonight. I can see it now: the double doors at the end of the church hall will fly open and I'll be standing there. I'll wait, just for a few seconds, looking round as if I'm deciding whether or not it's going to be worth my while staying. Adam will look up from his decks, his jaw will drop open and he'll go, 'Wow!' Then I'll walk across the hatch into the kitchen where there's going to be a soft drinks bar and I'll just stand with my back to the counter, leaning on one elbow and swigging from the bottle looking really cool. Ooh, whenever I think about it I go all goosepimply. I can't wait.

Arlette's coming round soon so that we can go through my wardrobe together – again! She's bringing a load of her stuff as well. My leopard print dress with the halter neck looks cool, but it doesn't go with my new shoes and, to be frank, I think animal print is a bit last centuryish – you know, a bit too 'Scary Spice'. I'm going more for the sophisticated look. Of course, if I did wear the silver crop top I could put on that fake tattoo and stick-on belly-button jewel – a ruby – that Auntie Venice gave me for my birthday. Oh, yes! Now that really would look excellent.

Was I Rasputin in a previous life or something? Have I committed some terrible sin that I have to be punished for? Life is so unfair!

OK, so everything was going great, right? Arlette had come round to mine at about five o'clock so that we'd have plenty of time. The disco was due to start at seven but only the truly sad cases (and the sound crew, of course, including Adam) would get there at the beginning. I was a bit miffed that Arlette disappeared round to Daniel's for about an hour and came back looking all red faced and sore-lipped – I really need to talk to her about being more cool. I mean, there we were getting all dressed up to go to the event of the year and she's standing there looking like a little kid who's been sucking a strawberry split. Honestly!

Anyway, we were both really excited trying on all these outfits – we even had to call Seema to come round with reinforcements. In the end we didn't need them though because it was a unanimous vote for the silver top with the tattoo and stick-on ruby. The new shoes were a little bit of a problem though. I've never worn any that were quite that high and it reminded me of when I was little and Dad drilled holes in a couple of hot-chocolate tins and threaded string through to make me some of those funny stilty-type things. The whole thing was a disaster because I couldn't co-ordinate the strings and I went over on my ankle. I remember grabbing for Gran but I accidentally smacked her in the mouth, knocked out her false teeth, then stumbled forwards on my hot-chocolate tins and broke her top set, before falling on the ground, twisting my ankle and grazing both knees. As you can imagine, it wasn't one of my happier experiences, so the sensation of tottering on my new shoes brought back all kinds of traumatic memories.

'Don't worry,' Seema said, grabbing my arm, 'you can hold on to us until we get there, and by that time you'll have got used to the altitude.'

'Let's have a look at you, love.' Gran came out of the sitting room as we were leaving. 'Very nice, but aren't you going to be a bit chilly?'

'I'll be fine, Gran.' I wanted to get out of the house before Dad could see me. Call it intuition but I had a sneaky suspicion that he wasn't going to go a bundle on my outfit. I wanted to make a hasty exit before he could launch into the whole 'cover yourself up', 'what is that in your navel?' and (most embarrassing of all) 'what time does it finish so that I can pick you up?' routine. I could hear Sirius scratching at the back door, so I gave Gran a quick kiss on the cheek and tried to make my escape.

'Is that you, Magenta?' Too late. He'd been in the

garden studying the stars. I don't know what he finds so interesting to look at but I keep hoping he'll spot something that might mean his mood's in the ascendancy at last. Honestly, my dad used to be an OK guy but the past few weeks it's like he's had a personality transplant or something. If Gran's having a late-life crisis, he's certainly doing the mid-life version. I sometimes think I'm the only sane person in my family.

'Traitor,' I whispered to Sirius, who'd obviously given me away. Then, 'Just going. Bye!' I grabbed Arlette and Seema and made a dash for the door. Well, not a dash exactly – not in my shoes – more a sort of a waddle. It was already eight o'clock and I didn't want to get there too late. Of course I didn't want to get there too early either. If I was going to make an entrance there would have to be quite a few people there already. However, if we hung around long enough for Dad to go through his whole KGB routine it would be kicking-out time before we even arrived.

'Hold on, I want to have a look at my little girl in all her finery.' Dad was smiling this really sickly false smile. He always tries to come across as 'Mr Reasonable' when my friends are around, but I knew he was going in for the kill. His eyes were focused on my navel area, so I shot Gran a pleading look.

'Come on, Curtis. Let these young things go out and enjoy themselves.'

'That's not . . .'

'Bye, girls,' said Gran, opening the door (It's wonderful what a guilty conscience can do, isn't it?)

'Take your coat,' Dad called. What time shall I pick you up?' and, as Gran closed the door, I could hear him saying, 'That isn't real, is it? Tell me she hasn't been mutilating her body . . .'

Off we went with arms linked. The three amigos! I'd like to tell you that linking arms was a symbol of the strength of our friendship – which of course it was – but actually it had more to do with the fact that I would probably have needed leg irons if Seema and Arlette hadn't been there to keep me in the upright position.

The youth club wasn't far and the nice thing is, it takes people from other schools too, so it's not always the same crowd. We go to Archimedes High. All the schools in our area are called after famous people but the other schools have got really cool names like Albert Einstein Academy and Germaine Greer High. I'm not sure what happened with us. All the others are named after really intellectual people, but we ended up being called after some ancient Greek carpenter – apparently he invented the screw of something but it all seems a bit manual to me. Anyway, kids from about three or four different schools go to the youth club so it's quite nice – most of the time.

When we arrived there was a gang of boys from Leonardo da Vinci just hanging outside. They were all a bit geekish but they started making all these comments like we were single or something. Well, I know I was on my own at that point, but the other two weren't. And I wasn't going to be on my own for long, I was convinced of that. (Little did I know how true that was going to turn out!)

'Hey, don't I know you?' one of them leered at Seema.

Then another grinned at Arlette. 'Hiya. You look gorgeous.'

I'm sure one of them was just about to say something to me when Seema challenged them. 'Did you say something? Or would you prefer to come inside and speak to my boyfriend?'

That shut them up.

I was a bit disappointed because the double doors were propped open and there were masses of people inside. I know Bruno had said we could bring friends – Bruno's the youth leader; this really cool guy who can eat fire and ride a unicycle and stuff – but this was seriously oversubscribed. I mean, we were talking sardines. So it wasn't so much a case of throwing open the door and standing framed in the doorway, as trying to squeeze through the crowd without suffering a cracked rib.

'Yoo hoo!' Arlette shrieked above the music (which I have to say was excellent, but then what would you expect with Adam DJ-ing?) 'I can see Daniel,' she shouted into my ear, as she waved in such a nerdy way it was practically social suicide to be seen with her.

Daniel pushed his way over to us and gave Arlette a peck on the cheek, then dragged her off in the direction of the stage where the DJ box was. The next thing I knew Seema had disappeared with Ben and I was left on my own. Honestly – call themselves friends!

I was determined to stick to my plan though. I wasn't going to look over to where I knew Adam was. I was going to stroll across to the hatch and get a drink. I made sure I was within sight of the stage where the DJs were though, just so that Adam could see me. Of course, with that many people, simply getting across the floor was like negotiating an assault course and with my new shoes it actually bordered on the extreme sports register. But I managed it.

Bruno had built a little counter out of tables in the corner and he was sitting on a silver unicycle, juggling crisps and drinks while Georgina, his assistant, was selling them. Talk about feeding time at the zoo! Honestly, you'd think Coke was rationed the way some people were acting. And, to make it worse, they didn't have any drinks in bottles, only cans, so any hope of swigging from the bottle and looking really cool and sophisticated went right out the window.

'Two cans to your right,' Georgie shouted. Bruno tossed two of the cans he was juggling over to the crowd on his right and everyone cheered when this little kid caught them. (To be honest, she didn't look old enough to be there – she was probably only just out of primary school.) Then Georgie threw two more into the air and Bruno carried on juggling. I just hoped he wasn't going to expect me to participate in his circus. I mean, it's OK for Year 7s and stuff like that, but it's a bit childish when you get to my age. So I just had a quiet word in Georgina's ear. I knew she'd understand.

Once I'd got my drink I wanted to make quite sure that Adam could see me. I went and sat by the edge of the stage. On the way over some little kid jogged my arm and I split my Coke right down my front. There was this long wet stain, like a dribble, down my silver top and it was all running down my tummy. Unfortunately, when I went to rub it off I also managed to rub off my stick-on ruby and it rolled off into the middle of the dance floor. And, to make matters worse some of the tattoo began to peel off too. I was beginning to get the distinct impression that things were not going to go exactly as planned.

'Hi, Magenta!' I looked round and Spud was standing behind me with a grin like a lump of Edam cheese in chicken wire.

I thought I'd better be polite, even though I didn't want him spoiling my chances with Adam, so I just gave him a casual, 'Oh, hi.'

I could see Daniel behind the mixing desk. He was sitting down and he had Arlette on his lap; she was laughing and giggling. (And making a bit of a fool of herself, if I'm going to be honest – I know she's my best friend but the way she's been behaving since she started going out with Daniel, it's as though she's been attending the Tragic School of Inane Behaviour.) I could see Joe as well; he was wearing headphones and trying to look majorly serious. But I couldn't see Adam.

'Are you with anyone?' It was Spud again. Aaagh! No way was I going to give him the impression I was available. I mean, I didn't want to be rude or anything but I thought it was better not to encourage him and to be honest right from the start.

'Yes, I am, actually,' I said. (I'm sure lying's OK as long as your *motives* are honest. And after all, I wasn't *really* lying because I *was* with Arlette and Seema. So if I gave him the impression I was with a *boy* it was just a little fib to save him from getting hurt.)

'Oh,' he said – and he looked really disappointed (which was quite sweet I thought).

Then I caught sight of Ben and Seema. 'Must go – sorry.' And I shot off and left him.

I certainly had no intention of playing gooseberry to Seema and Ben all night, but dancing with them was OK as an interim measure. I was still trying to catch a glimpse of Adam (and trying to avoid looking at Arlette and Daniel – yuk!), when who should walk up the steps on to the stage, carrying two cans of Coke, but Anthea Pritchard, with her nylon braids, and legs like beanpoles. And you should've seen what she was wearing! It was this tiny little gold crocheted thing that wouldn't even have been decent on the beaches of southern Europe! Honestly, what a slapper! But worse still, she put one of the cans down on a shelf at the back of the stage and then Adam stood up and drank from it. He'd been crouched down at the back all the time looking through the boxes of records.

'What's *she* doing here?' I asked Seema. 'She doesn't even come to this youth club.'

Seema shrugged. 'Do you really need to ask?' And she tossed her head in the direction of the stage.

I could not believe my eyes. The Pritch had her arms draped round Adam's neck and she was wriggling her hips like she'd got a dislocated pelvis or something. Then she pulled him towards her and got him in a full on lip-lock.

'Look what she's doing to Adam!' I shouted, pulling Seema and Ben apart.

Seema gave me this rather pitying look. 'It doesn't look as though he's objecting too much, if you ask me.'

I was gutted! Adam – my Adam – had fallen for the Pritch. What on Earth had possessed him? To be seduced by such obvious and tacky tricks! Surely it couldn't be true. She must have been snogging him against his will. I had another peek, but no – he was kissing her back. And without going into all the gory details, I was surprised that breathing apparatus wasn't required.

'Where are you going?' Seema called as I headed for the loos.

'Nowhere.' I was still trying to retain some of my dignity. But then as I was crossing the dance floor I saw Janet Dibner smooching with one of the boys from Leonardo da Vinci. Even Janet Dibner, the fashion guru from 1950, had managed to pull! It was more than I could bear. I went into the toilets and burst into tears.

'Madge?' I could hear Seema's voice as she pushed open one cubicle door after another. 'Magenta? Are you in here? Come on, speak to me.'

'No!' I said, before I realised that I'd given myself away.

Seema started banging on the door. 'Come on, open the door and let me in.'

'Go away!' I didn't want to talk to anyone. I'd have run home if I could've managed it without breaking an ankle. I certainly had no intention of allowing anyone to see me in my present state; I could probably do a passable impersonation of a panda and my face always went puce when I cried. (Not that I cry often, you understand.)

But Seema wasn't one to give up easily. 'Don't let him get to you. He's not worth it, you know.'

'Yes he is!' I wailed. 'I want to go home.'

'Well, if you really want to, I'll go and ring your dad to come and pick you up.'

'No!' How could she even think such a thing? If there was one thing worse than going out and facing everyone, it was admitting to Dad that tonight hadn't been a raging success. If I was going home, it would be under my own steam and not sitting in the passenger seat of the great I-told-you-so-mobile. 'I'll be OK in a minute,' I conceded. 'Have you got any tissues?'

I'll say this for Seema, when the chips are down she's always been really there for me and between the two of us, Kleenex and Max Factor, we made a fairly good attempt at damage repair.

'Now,' Seema said, patting a little dab of foundation over the blotches on my cheeks, 'go back out there and pull someone else. He's never going to go for you if he thinks you just hang around waiting for him. Go get him, jealous girl!'

'Yes!' And we slapped on it. I felt inspired. This was going to be the new plan. I was going to play the field; dance with as many boys as I could – right under Adam's nose! Oh, I couldn't wait.

'Hi, Magenta. Are you all right? You're not ill or anything are you?' It was Spud, standing outside the girls' loos. I gave him a quick once-over. Perhaps

Arlette was right – he wasn't so bad after all. And here he was, waiting for me, like the answer to my prayers.

'I'm fine thanks, Spud. Fancy a dance?' I grabbed his hand before he could answer and dragged him off to the front of the hall – right in front of the stage.

'Coo-ee!' Arlette waved at me, pointed at Spud and gave me the thumbs-up sign. Then she pointed in the direction of the decks. 'Look – Daniel's doing his set. Isn't he gorgeous?' she shrieked above the music.

Actually, I was quite impressed with his choice of music. But before I could get too engrossed, Spud began dancing. What a nightmare! It was as though he'd suddenly contracted mad spider disease. Arms and legs everywhere; head flying from side to side and up and down; hair and ears flapping like a maniac. I could feel my eyes almost popping out in horror. People had actually stopped dancing to stare at him. I had to do something; this was more embarrassing than Dad at Uncle Wayne's New Year's Eve party. In a moment of panic I put my hands on Spud's shoulders and started moving slowly.

'Oh, wow!' Spud put his hands on my waist and pulled me towards him – a little too close for comfort, actually. 'I think you're great, you know, Magenta.'

'Do you?' I said, trying to push him back to arm's length.

'And you know what?' It was fast becoming a game of push-me-pull-you; him pulling me closer and me pushing him away; in out, in out – but at least it was stopping Spud from shaking it all about.

'Go on, surprise me,' I said, not really thinking about what I might be inviting.

So he did! Before I knew what was happening he'd clasped both his arms round me in a sort of bear-hug and planted his mouth right over the top of mine. Ugh! I couldn't move. I tried tapping him on the back – you know, like wrestlers do when they want to break – but he didn't take any notice. I was looking over his shoulder trying to catch the attention of someone who might come to my assistance but all I got from Seema and Arlette was the thumbs-up again. The only one who looked remotely shocked was Daniel and he was just standing there gawping like a goldfish.

The further I tried to move my head back, the more Spud followed until I was bent so far backwards I was almost doing the crab (I knew my BAGA gymnastics badges would come in handy for something). I had this gut feeling that it was absolutely essential for me to keep my lips tightly shut (there was no way I was going to give him the impression I was enjoying this), and yet oxygen was starting to become an issue. Help! I was getting desperate. Maybe, I thought, if I just open my mouth a little bit – just to sort of equalise the pressure. I might be able to slip off sideways.

Big mistake! As I began to slide off Spud's lips, there was a sensation of scraping metal and then – jammed! It was impossible to move anywhere.

'Erp!' I tried to shout for help but my mouth was well and truly welded to Spud's.

It seemed to take him several seconds to realise that what I was displaying was not passion but abject panic, and then he followed suit. He began waggling his head like Sirius does when he's playing with a stick.

'Ng-o!' I shouted – well, mumbled really. It's very difficult to shout when your teeth are locked on to someone else's. 'Hhock ick!' (Which was supposed to be *stop it*.)

Then Spud said something, but the roof of your mouth isn't the best place for hearing things, so I haven't a clue what he said. After all, if we'd been meant to hear with our mouths, our ears would've been put behind our teeth and not on the sides of our heads, wouldn't they? But right at that moment

I'd got enough going on in front of my teeth without pondering the possibilities of evolutionary mutation.

We had to get across the floor to Bruno. He'd be able to sort us out. Quite how we were going to manage it, I wasn't sure, but I definitely wanted to get out of view of the stage. I shuffled us around.

'Sht-eck, shteck, shteck,' I spluttered as we did a sort of sideways march – my left foot and Spud's right foot moving together like Siamese twins who were joined at the mouth.

It was bad enough that people seemed to think I was snogging Spud; the last thing I wanted was for anyone to find out that we seemed to have been bonded at the brace. I thought that we'd managed to sneak off the floor without everyone noticing what had happened but our cover was blown the second the paramedics arrived. It seems that while I'd been locked in the loo, the little girl who'd caught the coke cans had slipped on what someone said was a red marble (oops! I wondered what had happened to my ruby) and it had caused a sort of domino effect in the centre of the hall. There'd been several twisted ankles and a suspected broken wrist apparently.

'What sort of an idiot bring marbles to a disco?' Bruno was ranting as all the injuries sat sobbing in the kitchen waiting for the ambulance. It was probably the only time I was glad I couldn't speak.

So here we are in Casualty waiting for the on-call orthodontist to come over from the hospital dental school. It seems that the rubber bands on Spud's brace have got hooked on to my railtrack. (I don't know how I let myself get talked into dancing with him in the first place. This is all Seema's fault.)

The staff dealt with all the little kids first – which I'm not disputing. It's just that I could have done without them walking past us with that sort of smug serves-you-right type expression on their faces. I mean it's not like I was locked on to someone deliciously hunky or anything – this is Sam Pudmore, for heavens' sake. And as if the humiliation wasn't bad enough, I'm now developing seriously lacerated lips!

Dad's just arrived and, despite the caring-parent act he's putting on for the doctors, I can tell from the set of his eyes that there's an explosion like Vesuvius simmering away below the surface. I just hope Gran will still be awake when we get home. I was thinking that, as soon as I'd got the use of my mouth back, I'd kill Spud first and then maybe myself. But, by the look on Dad's face, I think he's going to save me the bother on both counts.

7
Daniel

Before you say anything, I'm not exactly proud of how I've behaved, OK? And in my defence, I didn't realise at the time just what a rat I was being.

When Magenta first asked me if I'd go out with Arlette I just thought, cool – what a brilliant way of getting Magenta jealous and showing her that I'm not a total loser on the girlfriend front. I suppose it didn't really occur to me that Arlette might actually really like me. Big mistake! I've now got nearly every girl in Year 9 on my case, Arlette snotting down the phone practically every night and Magenta, the object of my desire and the whole reason for going out with Arlette in the first place, won't even speak to me! So my first attempt to launch myself as a babe-magnet has completely backfired. Plus, my brother is on the warpath – in fact, he's so far along the warpath that he's practically knocking at Mr War's front door. I'm just laying low for a while because it'll only take one more step from Joe and this might be the last thing I ever write. But actually it doesn't matter, because if these are the best years of my life then I may as well die now.

It's not that I don't *like* Arlette, you understand. I mean, she's pretty and she's nice to talk to and everything, it's just that I don't go all weak at the knees when I think of her, like I do with Magenta. And, call me old-fashioned, but it didn't seem quite right for me to have the hots for my girlfriend's best friend.

It all came to a head a couple of weeks ago on the night of the youth club disco. When I saw Magenta kissing Spud like that (I can hardly bear to think about it even now) it was probably the worst moment of my life. I could hardly believe what I was seeing. It was like I was in a time-warp; I was frozen to the spot and everyone else was moving in slow motion – including Arlette who was jumping up and down on the stage next to me, giving Magenta the thumbs-up and screaming, 'Go for it, girl!' And I thought, she's Magenta's best friend so Magenta must have told her that she fancies Spud. And that must mean that Magenta doesn't fancy me! I was gutted.

We'd lived next door to each other for ten years, since just after Magenta's mum died, and I'd been hoping, since about Year 6, that one day we might be an item. But the painful truth was staring me in the face. And apart from that, Spud was supposed to be my mate and he certainly knew how I felt about Magenta. Yet there he was, snogging the love of my life right in front of my eyes. And not only that, but he was snogging her so passionately that their mouths had got welded together. I couldn't bear it.

'Daniel, you plonker!' It wasn't till Joe thumped me on the back that I realised I'd forgotten about the next record. 'Some music might be a good idea – seeing as how this is supposed to be a disco.' It had been my set and I'd been really on top of it, doing the mixing the way Adam had taught me but then I realised that everything had gone quiet. All these kids were staring up at the DJ box, just waiting. I was so engrossed in watching Magenta and Spud doing this sort of side-step off the dance floor that I'd completely lost it. Adam and Joe were furious – Arlette wasn't looking too pleased with me, either.

That night I couldn't sleep. I didn't know why I felt so screwed up but at about two o'clock in the morning I heard Curtis' car pull up outside as he and Magenta got back from the hospital. I could hear him ranting on and on, yet I didn't feel remotely sorry for her. I just thought, you deserve everything you get, Magenta Orange!

I went down to make a cup of tea and Mum must've heard me. 'Want to talk about it?' My mum's all right when it comes to listening to problems. She's got all these books on relationships and stuff – not that it did her and Dad much good, but still. Mum's a nurse and my dad was a professional footballer. They met when he injured his knee and had to have an operation, but they got divorced just after I was born. Mum says she's a nurse who lost her patients! Never mind, let's go back to the small hours of Saturday morning a couple of weeks ago.

So there I was, pouring it all out. (What is it about the middle of the night that seems to make you do strange, out-of-character things?) When I'd finished rambling, Mum just looked at me.

'What goes around, comes around,' she said, but not in a smug way.

'What d'you mean?'

'Well, it seems to me that what Spud's done to you isn't so very different from what you've been doing to Arlette.'

I thought she must have been at the gin or something, because I couldn't see the similarity at all. I mean, I hadn't gone and snogged someone Arlette fancied, had I?

'No, but you've been going out with Arlette when it's really her best friend you fancy, isn't it?'

It was true! Oh my God, what a slimeball I'd been!

What a total and utter worm! How could I live with myself? I was going to have to sell myself into penal servitude for the rest of my life to make amends.

'Well, I think that's a *little* drastic,' Mum smiled, 'but perhaps a bit of honesty wouldn't go amiss?'

Honesty? Now she was scaring me. 'How can I be honest? What am I supposed to say – oh by the way, Arlette, I've only been going out with you to get your best friend jealous?'

Mum gave me one of those looks that parents do when you know you've said something extremely stupid or childish. 'I said honesty, Daniel, not brutality. There's no law that says we have to tell the whole truth the whole time. Just do the honest thing. Finish with Arlette and tell her that it doesn't feel right for you, or it's not what you're looking for, or something like that. Just be sensitive – I'm sure you can manage that.'

It sounded so easy when Mum said it – I would just tell Arlette that this wasn't what I was looking for – piece of cake – NOT!

I spent the whole weekend hiding out in my bedroom, avoiding everyone.

'Daniel!' I even pulled down the blinds so that Magenta couldn't see into my room and disturb me. 'Daniel, I know you're in there 'cos I can hear your music through the wall. Let me in, I need to talk to you.' It was the first time in my life I'd not wanted to see Magenta – whatever was going on with me must be serious. 'Don't make me have to use the front door, Daniel.' I kept very quiet. I didn't want to talk to anyone.

A few minutes later Mum came up to my room.

'Tell her I'm doing an essay,' I said.

Mum ruffled my hair like she used to do when I was about three. 'I know it's hard, love, but I'm sure you'll do the right thing.'

The right thing! What was 'the right thing'? Was it really better to finish with Arlette just because I fancied Magenta more? Or should I concentrate on Arlette's good points and try to make a go of it? This was my first trip into the world of relationships and after only two weeks I was a total mess! Why on Earth did adults bother? I was going to stay single for ever. And it was true I had an essay to write – not that I could focus on anything. Every time I put my pen on the page a stream of *Magenta, Magenta, Magenta* came out and nothing whatsoever about the reasons for the destruction of the Brazilian rainforests. I wasn't even interested in my computer. I just lay on my bed staring up at the poster of Sarah Michelle Gellar that was stuck to my ceiling – just a little bit torn after the night the blu-tack came unstuck and I woke up having a nightmare that I was fighting off this enormous crinkly octopus that was trying to smother me. Life sucks.

By Monday morning I'd decided to do the decent thing and let Arlette down gently. I thought it was best to wait until after school though – I had the distinct impression that she wasn't going to take too kindly to the break-up and I didn't want her to dis me all round school. Arlette's bus stops right outside the main gate so, if I was going to avoid her, my best bet was to go in early so that if she hung around at the bus stop she wouldn't see me. Then I'd find something to do at lunchtime and break up with her on the way home so that she'd got all evening to get over it.

'Oh no, you don't!' Mum had grabbed the collar of my jacket and was heaving me back into the house.

'But Mum, I need to be in early today.'

'You also need to clear the table and do the washing-up.' She yanked my bag off my shoulder and pushed a pile of plates into my hand. 'You know we all have to pull our weight in this household.'

'Aw, Mum! I'll do it tonight as soon as I get home, I promise. But I really do have to be in early this morning.'

'Daniel, it's twenty to eight. It takes you approximately five minutes to walk to school. The only person who'll be there at this time is the caretaker, so unless you have an arrangement to go in and sweep the floors, I don't think you're being entirely honest with me.' (My mum's going through a bit of an honesty spree at the moment.) She looked at me like she had X-ray vision or something. 'So, which one are you trying to avoid – Arlette or Magenta?'

It's funny, but at half past two in the morning, under the influence of sleep deprivation, she'd seemed quite sympathetic; in the cold light of the first day back after the half term holiday she seemed about as sympathetic as Attila the Hun. I was just about to argue with her when Joe walked in, looking like he'd had a night getting wrecked with Godzilla.

'Oooo – look at eager-beaver Danny-boy. Can't wait to get back and see little Miss Too-Cool-For-School Magenta.' He took a bite of cold toast and grinned this crummy grin right in my face. 'Oh no, I forgot – Magenta's not your girlfriend, is she? You're going out with her best friend, you Casanova, you! Tell me, Danno, what're you going to call yourself at the next disco – DJ Romeo and the Sound of Silence?'

'Just 'cos you haven't got a girlfriend!' I know it

was childish, but he really gets up my nose sometimes.

'Is that right?' Joe was looking really smug like he knew something that I didn't.

'Boys! That's enough!' Mum was putting on her lipstick. (Why she had to wear make-up to go looking after a load of sick people I've never known.) 'If you can't be civil to each other, then don't speak at all. And Daniel, I don't want you to leave before you've done all the washing-up and made sure your room's tidy.'

So that meant that by the time I eventually left home I was just passing the bus stop when I heard this: 'Yoo hoo! Daniel!' My heart sank. It was Arlette. 'Where've you been?' She put both her arms round my neck and tried to plant this great big smacker on my lips.

'Not here, Arl,' I said, pulling away.

'Someone got out of bed the wrong side this morning, didn't they?' she said, chirpily. I felt sick. 'Why didn't you phone me yesterday? I left three messages.' She clutched my arm and snuggled up to me. It was like torture. What a toad I was being.

'I had to finish my geography essay.' My fingers were tightly crossed behind my back.

Arlette looked slightly hurt, then she smiled.

'Friday was brilliant, wasn't it?'

It was more than I could bear. 'Look, Arlette, I've got to go now. Catch you later.'

'Daniel?' She stood there, looking puzzled.

I was just relieved that we were in different tutor groups so it was unlikely that our paths would cross during the day. I made sure I steered clear of the yard at break and at lunchtime I offered to help Ms Lovell tidy the Art room. Ms Lovell's really cool. She was telling me that she does this meditation thing called Tai Chi.

'Wow!' I said, somewhat amazed. 'What a co-incidence. My next-door neighbour does a thing called Tai Chi too but his is a martial art – are they related, do you think?'

She smiled. 'Tai Chi is a martial art, but it's also meditation through motion and stillness.' Then she gave me this funny, knowing sort of look. 'Is that Magenta Orange's father?'

How creepy is that! Surely teachers have got better things to do than discuss which pupils live where. 'How did you know that Magenta was my next-door neighbour?'

'I'm not sure.' She looked a bit sheepish. 'Perhaps Magenta mentioned it at some point. I take her group as well.'

Wow! Magenta had talked to Ms Lovell about me! Maybe there was hope after all. I started to tell her about how Curtis practises in the garden, looking like he's doing this sort of slow-motion dance thing. And how Sirius, Magenta's dog, sometimes thinks Curtis is playing and leaps on to his slipper growling and refusing to let go. So Curtis is out there all serious-faced, balancing on one leg with this little dog flapping about on the end of his foot!

As I was telling her, Ms Lovell's face creased up into this big smile and she looked really pretty but then suddenly she went all sad. 'I think it's time you went for your lunch now, Daniel,' she said. 'Thank you for helping.' And I thought she was going to burst into tears.

I don't understand women. I mean, I thought I was telling a funny story but if it had that sort of effect on Ms Lovell, heaven knows what sort of effect finishing with Arlette will have on her. I decided to rethink my whole 'honest' policy. Maybe it would be better just to keep out of Arlette's way until she got fed up and either went off me or dumped me. Brilliant! I thought. So that's what I did. I arranged to stay late after Science and tidy up the labs on Monday. On Tuesday lunchtime it was the PE cupboard and, after school, the Geography stockroom. On Wednesday,

I spent the lunch-hour carting computers between classrooms for Mr Kingston. I was fast earning myself the name of Dan, Dan the Cleaning Man.

The crunch came that evening, after school. On Wednesdays we have Food Technology last lesson, which I'd thought was a pretty sure bet for at least an hour's cleaning of cookers and worktops.

'No thank you, Daniel,' Mrs Delaney said, bustling about in her pink apron. 'We have technicians for that.'

'But . . .'

'No buts. We teachers are not entirely devoid of our brains, Daniel. The rumour in the staffroom is that if you carry on the way you have been so far this week, the school budget will be several thousand pounds better off because we'll be able to sack the cleaners. Now, I'm not normally one to refuse an offer of assistance but something tells me there's more to this than meets the eye, so I suggest you go home tonight at the normal time and deal with whatever it is you're trying to avoid.' I might be wrong but I'm sure a few of her boils burst while she was sounding off at me.

There was no way I was ready to deal with Arlette so I hid between Mr Crusham's car and the shrubbery in the car park. He never leaves until about midnight so I was pretty sure I'd be safe until long after everyone else had gone.

'Have you seen Daniel?' I could hear Arlette's voice so I crouched down even lower.

Magenta answered and, I have to say, her tone was less than friendly. 'No, I haven't. And I don't want to either!' There! That confirmed my worst fears – Magenta really hated me. I was devastated. I noticed she was still talking with a bit of a lisp after Friday night – it made her sound so sweet.

Arlette piped up again. 'I'm sure he's not really avoiding you, Madge. There's probably some really simple explanation.' Oh no! Magenta thought it was *her* I was avoiding. I wanted to leap up from my hiding place and tell her, but I couldn't without Arlette seeing me.

And then, 'Hi, Spud. Have you seen Daniel anywhere?'

I'd primed Spud, so I was just praying he wouldn't let me down. 'I think he had to go home early.' Good old Spud.

'Don't you come within ten yardth of me, Tham Pudmore!'

'I said I was sorry, didn't I?' Sam sounded a bit pissed off.

'Thorry! Thorry? You think *thorry* ith going to

make up for the humiliathon you put me through?'

'It was just as embarrassing for me, you know.'

'Embarrathing for *you*?'

'Yes! Embarrassing. There's not a lot of street cred in getting your face fused on to someone else's, you know.' I didn't know what Spud was moaning about – I'd have given anything to have had some facial fusion with Magenta. Some people just don't know when they're well off.

Just at that moment I heard a clunk, like you get with central locking, and felt a shudder from The Crusher's car. There were two almost simultaneous slammings of the car doors and then the whole car began to vibrate as the engine started up. Just my luck that the only time this term he was leaving before nightfall was the time I was using his car for cover. I was crouched down between the radiator grille and an enormous laurel bush, which didn't offer a lot of scope for scrambling through, so it was only a matter of time before I was caught in the headlights like a prisoner trying to escape from Alcatraz.

'Davis! What the hell do you think you're doing tinkering with my car?' They caught me in a pincer movement, The Crusher on one side and Mr Onanije, the deputy head on the other.

'I wasn't tinkering with anything,' I told him.

'So what were you doing then?' I didn't have Mr Onanije for any lessons so I'd never really come into contact with him before.

'Nothing, sir.'

'Nothing!'

'It's all right, Samson,' The Crusher said. (Samson! Mr Onanije was called Samson? Wait till I divulged this extremely valuable piece of information to the rest of the form.) 'I'll deal with this. My office first thing in the morning, Davis!'

'It's OK, Daniel, I've found them!' Arlette was running up to me, grinning and shaking a bunch of keys.

'Uh?' I had no idea what was going on.

She turned to the gruesome twosome and beamed. 'I lost my keys and I thought I'd dropped them this morning when Ms Bignell asked me to put some equipment in her car for her, but I've found them now. Thanks, Daniel – you're a star!' Then she linked arms with me, kissed my cheek and off we walked towards the main gate. And the amazing thing was, she didn't even ask me what I'd been doing scrambling about in the herbaceous borders. Phew!

No such luck with Magenta though. We were walking home after leaving Arlette at the bus stop. 'Daniel, what are you playing at?'

I tried to act dumb.

'Are you avoiding me?'

'No!' I said with heartfelt honesty.

'Well, then you must be avoiding Arlette.'

'No-oooo.' I tried to muster the same degree of truth, but didn't quite succeed.

She was furious. 'If you're trying to do that *boy thing* of being tho horrible that the girl finithes with you, then you're more pathethic than I thought you were!' Suddenly her lisp didn't seem so appealing – in fact, it was about as attractive as Donald Duck throwing a wobbler.

'What d'you mean?' I bluffed. I was beginning to think that I'd turned into Transparency-Man or something. How is it that everyone seems to be able to see right through me?

'I mean, Daniel, if you're going to dump Arlette, just dump her. She detherveth to know the troof.' And she went inside and slammed her front door.

So that made up my mind. I had to do it. Magenta had used the dreaded 'P' word and there was no way I was letting her think I was pathetic.

So, on Thursday, I arranged to meet Arlette at *The Filling Station* – this cool little sandwich bar in the High Street. It's all done out like an American petrol station from the 1950s and they stay open into the evenings too.

'I'll pay.' It was the guilt of the executioner offering to pay for the condemned man's last meal. 'What're you having?'

'Ooo, how exciting!' Arlette was rubbing her hands in delight. I couldn't bear to watch. 'I'll have a large slice of Vegetable Supreme pizza and a blueberry smoothie, please – with a portion of chips.'

Eeek! I'd actually been thinking more in terms of a bag of crisps and a cup of tea. In economic terms she'd just spent an entire car wash and polish plus interior hoovering. But I forked out anyway. It seemed the least I could do in the circumstances.

'Arlette . . .' I stared, as she sucked on her smoothie.

'This is amazing! You sure you don't want anything?' She grinned at me and took hold of my hand across the table. 'You're so sweet,' she smiled. 'I'm really glad you suggested this. I was beginning to think I'd done something to upset you.'

I felt sick. It felt like a whole nestful of worms was wriggling about in my stomach. This was horrendous. Why hadn't I done this over the phone?'

'Arlette, there's something I want to talk to . . .'

'Oh my God! I don't believe it!' She was staring

towards the door. 'Don't look.'

The seating in *The Filling Station* was arranged in booths and the backs were quite high and made to look like petrol pumps. We were sitting in a booth close to the front. Arlette was facing the door and I was facing the counter and from the expression of astonishment on her face, I was missing something big.

'What is it? Tell me.' I was desperate to see what she was looking at and then, through the reflection in the chrome counter, all was revealed. It was my brother Joe. And he wasn't alone.

'Is that ...?' I whispered. Finishing with Arlette went completely out of the window.

She nodded excitedly. 'This is mega news! Can you imagine the effect this is going to have when it gets out?'

Unfortunately I could. My brother Joe was tongue-wrestling with Anthea Pritchard, the girlfriend of Adam Jordan. And, from what I knew of Adam, he wasn't going to take too kindly to the news – if anyone was stupid enough to tell him. And, more importantly for me, from what I knew of Joe, if he found out that I'd seen them I might as well donate my body to medical science now.

I shuffled into the corner of the seat and tried to

keep a low profile. 'Don't let them see us. Get down,' I whispered, as urgently as I could.

Too late. I looked up from my position, eye-balling the salt and pepper pots, to see Joe pointing his finger at me. 'One word and you're dead meat – understand?' Then he looked at Arlette and gave a sickly smirk. 'But you wouldn't dare say anything, would you, little bruv?'

Before I could reply, he looked at Anthea (who was pulling this lump of gum into a long string and then winding it back into her mouth with her tongue), tossed his head in the direction of the door and said, 'Come on, babe. Let's get out of here.'

Arlette was sitting with her mouth wide open. 'I cannot *wait* to tell Magenta. This is so majorly news-breaking.'

'Arlette!' I couldn't believe it. Didn't she have any thoughts for my welfare? 'You mustn't say anything to anyone.'

She looked upset – but only for a split second and then she punched the air like she'd just scored a winning goal or something. 'Oh yes! That is so cool! I know something Magenta doesn't – and she doesn't even *know* that she doesn't know! How brilliant is that?'

We stayed until Arlette had finished her pizza but

after that I just wanted to go home. She didn't stop talking about Joe and Anthea. She didn't seem to have any concept of the nuclear fall-out from the episode and how I was likely to die a slow painful death at the hands of my own brother and his Year 11 mafia. I know I hadn't actually got round to finishing with her (again!) but I just wasn't in the mood. So once I'd walked her back to her house, I made a decision: I really would finish with her tomorrow – after school – definitely.

The trouble is, I didn't get the chance – well, not in the nice, let-her-down-gently kind of way that I'd wanted. It ended up more as a horrible, harsh, blow-her-up-angrily in a volcanic-eruption kind of way.

You see, I just do not understand girls. One minute they're all giggly and chatty and telling each other everything. Then the next minute Arlette's scoring points because she knows something her best friend doesn't. And then, in the time it took me to get back from Arlette's, which couldn't have been more than twenty minutes, the phone wires have gone into overdrive (with, I might add, callous disregard for my life) and we're back to the gossipy all-girls-together routine. I mean, how is a boy supposed to know what he's dealing with?

'Daniel! Daniel!' Magenta was out on her balcony,

apparently waiting for me to get home. 'Come up and tell me all about it!'

'What?' I asked, still believing in the myth of female confidentiality.

'You know – about Joe and The Pritch.'

'How ... you ... she ...' I was gobsmacked. 'Wait there!' I ran upstairs and almost fell out of my bedroom and into Magenta's. 'I told Arlette not to say anything. How could she do this?'

Magenta was sitting cross-legged on her bed and bouncing up and down like a little kid who could hardly contain herself. 'Well, she only told me and she swore me to secrecy. Oooo – it's exciting, isn't it?'

'Exciting? What, exactly, is exciting about me being on my brother's hit list?'

'Well, not that, but the whole business about The Pritch two-timing and Joe cheating on his mate. It's juicy.'

There was something about the way she said *juicy* that set my alarm bells ringing. 'You haven't said anything to anyone else, have you?'

She bit her bottom lip and screwed up her nose. 'Only Seema. And she doesn't count because she's one of us – and anyway I've sworn her to secrecy.' She looked so lovely, it was difficult to be angry with her. 'And Candy,' she added, ''cos she was round at

Seema's when I rang – but we've sworn her to secrecy too.'

'Candy! Not Candy Meekin whose brother's in Year 11 and plays basketball for the school and is about seven feet nine tall and is a mate of Adam Jordan?' I was suddenly finding it quite easy to be angry with her. 'This is serious, Magenta!'

If Adam found out that his girlfriend was dating my brother, he was going to be furious and I was going to get slaughtered. If Joe found out that Adam had found out, I was going to get slaughtered because my brother's a meathead. It didn't seem fair that I would be on the receiving end of all that slaughtering simply because of an accident of birth. And, actually, it wasn't that that was bothering me. What was really freaking me out was that Joe might tell Magenta that I fancied her and that I'd only gone out with Arlette to get her jealous. If Magenta ever found out what a snake I'd been it would ruin my chances forever.

So it was crucial that Adam Jordan never found out. I wasn't sure how I was going to accomplish that but one thing was certain – I was going to deal with Arlette and her big mouth there and then.

'It's over, Arlette! Finished! Finito! The End.'

'I'm sorry. I didn't mean to – it just sort of slipped

119

out.' She was blubbing buckets – I could hear.

One part of me felt really horrible but there was another part that was humungously relieved. 'It didn't just slip out, Arlette, you just couldn't wait to blab it all over the school. Your foot couldn't have been more than a centimetre over the doorstep before you picked up the phone. You must have arms like Inspector Gadget to have got to it so quickly. Well, I mean it – it's over.' And I put the phone down.

Wow! I felt like Sylvester Stallone – firm and manly. That was the way to do it.

But five minutes later, 'Daniel! How could you?' Magenta was raging outside my French window. 'Let me in. Arlette's really upset.'

'I'm tired. I want to go to sleep.'

'Sleep! How can you think of sleeping when your girlfriend's crying her heart out over you?'

Was I imagining things, or hadn't Magenta told me to finish with Arlette? And now she was mad because I had. I've said it before and I'll say it again – I do not understand girls!

'She isn't my girlfriend any more. Now leave me alone.'

Then old Mrs Pickles across the road came to my rescue. 'Will you stop all that caterwauling over there. It's turned ten o'clock and decent folks is trying to get some sleep.'

I heard Magenta close her window and I lay back and stared up at Sarah Michelle. 'I will speak to you about this tomorrow,' I heard her shout through the wall.

But she didn't.

In fact, that was a week ago and she hasn't spoken to me since. Neither has Arlette, except to ring up every night and cry – but that doesn't count as speaking to me. Joe just sort of growls threateningly if we happen to meet on the stairs or across the dining table – which is an improvement on his normal level of conversation, I suppose.

But the worst thing of all is Adam Jordan. It seems that Magenta, not being a girl to miss an opportunity, took it upon herself to tell Adam what sort of a two-timing skunk he was dating. And now every time I go into the dining hall all I see is the two of them, Adam and Magenta, sitting next to each other and Magenta going all giggly every time he opens his mouth. Talk about pass the chuck-bucket!

There was an advert on television last night for the Army. I wonder how old I need to be to get into the SAS? That would show them all.

8
Magenta

I am so excited! I can hardly believe it. I am going on a date!

Now, I'm going to tell you something that not many people know – it's not something I care to shout about, if you know what I mean – but, actually, this is my first proper date. I mean, apart from going to the Year 6 Christmas party with Daniel but that doesn't count because:

a) we were only Year 6 and I was too immature to know my own mind, and

b) Daniel is a total dork and I'm not speaking to him (I'll explain all about that later). But the most exciting bit is (are you ready?) . . .

MY DATE IS WITH ADAM JORDAN!

How fantastic is that? Oooo, I go shuddery all over when I think about it. He's going to meet me outside the Roxy Cinema at six o'clock. I know that sounds a bit early but you would not believe the hassle I've had getting Dad to agree to this. To start with he put his size tens down and said I couldn't go at all. Talk about coming on the heavy parent! But let me go back over the last week because it's all been a bit of a dream, really.

It turns out that Adam's two-timing ex-girlfriend, Anthea Slapper Pritchard was cheating on him with his supposed mate, Daniel's double-crossing brother, Joe. I felt so sorry for poor Adam. It's not nice to have things going on behind your back, is it? So I decided that it was my duty to put him out of his misery. I mean, imagine what he would've felt like if he'd just happened to bump into them, like Arlette and Daniel did? It would've been terrible for him. And he was so grateful that I told him – well, not at first. He was fuming at first. He stormed out of the dining hall like a bull with a migraine. And then I'm not really sure what happened next because Daniel would normally have been my informant but I'm not speaking to him. I think he treated Arlette despicably. (I'm so glad Arl taught me that word, I use it all the time now – especially around Daniel – the rat.)

The other thing that really upset me though is that Arlette isn't speaking to *me*. Can you believe that? She's got some half-brained idea that it was *my* fault that Daniel finished with her.

'I told you not to tell anyone, Magenta, but you just had to go blabbing it all round the school!'

'Come on, Arl. You know that's not true. I only

told Seema and if anyone can keep a secret, she can.' I couldn't bear to hear her so upset, so I thought it best not to mention the unfortunate Candy Meekin slip. It was just one of those freaky accidents that happens sometimes. I didn't *mean* to tell the whole world, but Candy was round at Seema's when I rang up bursting with all the goss from Arlette. In fact, I was so excited that Seema was in danger of getting a ruptured eardrum and had to hold the phone away from her ear. And that's how it happened. Granted, Candy is about as diplomatic as the front page of your average tabloid newspaper and her brother, Sherman, who has a physique like an armour-plated double-decker bus, is in Year 11 and a mate of Adam's. But I didn't even know she was there until it was too late: it's so unfair that Arlette blames me.

Anyway, back to Adam – gorgeously understanding and wonderfully grateful person that he is. I have to admit, he did act a bit weird for a couple of days after I'd told him about The Pritch cheating on him, so when I heard his voice on Thursday, I could hardly believe my ears.

'Hey, why don't you come and join us?' As you know, my history with Adam has not been entirely free from misunderstanding, so I did a double take, just in case. But it was true – Adam Jordan was inviting me to sit with him and his gang of friends – who, by the way, are all in Year 11. I was, like, *so* flattered.

There was a teensy little bit of a downer when he said, 'I can't remember what you said your name was.'

And one of his mates came up with, 'It's some colour isn't it? Maroon or something.'

But then, get this, right – I was so proud of myself. I just stood there and said, 'Magenta, actually. Not Maroon, or Scarlet, or Crimson, or Puce. It's Magenta!' And I stared him out, like I do with Dad when he threatens to stop my pocket money. Talk about Girl-Power!

There was this, 'WooooOOooo!' from his mates and then Adam smiled this absolutely fantastic smile – right into my eyes.

'Cool name.' And he patted the seat next to him for me to go and sit down.

It was like, hello, somebody pinch me, because reality has never been this good. Adam Jordan – THE Adam Jordan, the boy I've fancied since the beginning of term – had finally seen the light! Oh, it was so fantastic; my insides went completely to jelly. Of course I was a teensy bit mad that Arlette and Seema weren't there to witness my big moment.

Seema was doing her best to talk some sense into Arlette but Arl can be very stubborn at times. I'm pretty sure I saw Daniel come into the dining hall and I think he saw me, although I can't be certain because he walked straight out again. But then there was this deliciously satisfying moment when Miss Terminally-Brain-Dead herself, Anthea I-wouldn't-know-loyalty-if-it-jumped-up-and-split-the-ends-of-my-synthetic-hair-extensions Pritchard, came into the dining hall. Honestly, the way she walks, she's like a cross between a *Thunderbirds* puppet and a chicken – an absurdly long-legged chicken at that. I bet she thought she was being so sophisticated as she made a point of walking past our table and sitting at the next one without looking at Adam. But, actually, she looked like a total jerk and, I'm ashamed to say, there was a little bit of me that wished she'd trip up.

'I really appreciate what you did, you know.' Adam had his elbow on the table and he was sort of sprawled out, looking right at me, as though I was the only person in the world. Goose-bump city, or what! Then he said to me, in this gorgeously husky voice, 'So, Magenta . . .' The way he says my name is soooo wonderful: he puts a sort of sigh on the end, like *Magent-ah*. But then I lost the plot a bit because I was so busy going all dreamy about him saying my name that I didn't quite catch the end of the sentence. It sounded like he was asking me if I fancied some liniment for Saturday's fight.

'What?'

He shrugged. 'OK then. No pressure.'

'No, no!' I started to panic. 'I just didn't catch what you said.' If Adam Jordan wanted me to provide liniment for some fight or other on Saturday, then I was up for it – even though, strictly speaking, I don't approve of fighting or violent sports like boxing and netball.

'I asked you,' he said in a really loud voice, like I'd got some sort of hearing deficiency, 'if you fancied coming to the cinema on Saturday night?'

Wow! This was so mega – and there was no one there to see me being asked out by Mr Drop-Dead-Gorgeous himself. Typical! One person who *had* witnessed it though was The Pritch because she got up and gave her hair a flick, like a horse twitching its tail, and stomped off in her disjointed, *Thunderbirds*-y way. That showed her!

Of course, as it turns out, actually *getting* the date was the easy part – convincing my dad that I was not going to end up on the next month's edition of *Crimewatch* was a different matter.

'Mother . . .' Gran is much more persuasive than I am, so I'd decided to let her talk Dad round. And also, she knows that I could still drop her and Auntie Vee in it over the whole motorbike malarkey, so I thought that would give more of an edge to her argument.

I was standing in the hall with my ear pressed against the kitchen door. I had to practically gag Sirius to stop him whining and giving me away but, I have to say, I was a tad surprised at the amount of resistance Dad was putting up.

'No! Absolutely no way!' He was using his strained-but-reasonable voice and saying things in separate syllables like Gran was some sort of alien who didn't understand English. '. . . she-is-thir-teen-years-old.'

Honestly, anyone would think I was still in nappies the way my dad goes on. I mean thirteen is practically a woman – according to old Bonesie, in medieval times girls got married at my age. I bet *their* fathers didn't try to stop them going to the cinema!

'Yes, Curtis, she's thirteen. She's growing up.' Good old Gran. She really is a legend in her own leather jacket. 'You can't keep her wrapped up in cotton-wool. She's a sensible girl and it's not as though they're going to the late night showing. She'll be home by nine o'clock.'

Nine o'clock! That came as a bit of a shocker. But when I thought about it, Gran was right; I am a sensible girl. And if agreeing to get home by nine was what it took to get Dad's approval, then I was happy to go along with that. Anyway, who knows what might happen? Just because I agree to be home at nine, doesn't mean it'll necessarily be possible for that to happen. Circumstances change all the time, don't they?

'Very well, then,' I heard Dad say. I could hardly believe it. Yes! I gave Sirius a big cuddle and let him lick my face – prematurely, as it turns out. 'But only on condition that I gave her a lift there and back.' Aaaaagh! I knew there had to be a catch. *No way* was he going to chaperone me! Can you imagine the humiliation on Monday? What is it with adults that they give you something and then snatch it away again, practically in the same breath?

'Come on now, Curtis. How old were you when you took Sheila Hogbin to that barn dance at the community centre? Twelve? Thirteen?'

Sheila Hogbin? A barn dance? What was this grossly sordid past my father had been hiding?

'I was nearly fourteen and that was different.'

It always is with adults, isn't it?

'Well, in my book, nearly fourteen means thirteen, and I wonder how you'd have felt if your father had insisted on driving you there.'

Dad went ranting on and on. 'It was different then . . .' Blah, blah, blah. And on and on . . . So I sat down in the hall keeping quiet and hoped Gran would do her stuff. Eventually he did come round – I think it was the memory of Sheila Hogbin that did it for him – good old Gran. It was a compromise though – I had to agree to be home by nine. I was sure Adam would understand. He's so lovely.

Talk about panic stations! The biggest day of my life comes along and Arlette (my supposed best friend) was still refusing to speak to me! Can you believe it? She can be so unreasonable sometimes. Personally, I blame Daniel. He never thinks about anyone but himself.

It was a real bummer actually, because Arl has this fantastic lime green dress she bought in the summer and I had my heart set on borrowing it. It's not exactly the same colour as my shoes but almost, and I thought if I wore my little black fluffy cardigan with it, it would look great. I mean, it's so important to get things right on a first date, isn't it? Not too formal, not too casual. And Arlette's dress would've been perfect. I was really peed off with her – she was making such a drama out of this whole thing with Daniel. Apart from all the time Seema had spent last week trying to talk her round, she'd been on the phone to Arl for most of this morning as well. And just when I was thinking she'd succeeded and should be awarded the Nobel Peace Prize, Arlette came round to my house and tossed this green top at me that looked like it had just dropped off a Day-Glo Christmas tree.

'My dress is in the wash, so I've brought this.' She had her arms folded and a definite hint of a sulk on her face – like she was doing me this huge favour. (Which, I'll admit, she would've been if she'd brought the dress.) 'It's Cassie's but she left it behind when she went to Uni.'

I could not believe my eyes. If I tell you that Arlette's sister Cassie putts the shot for the County Under-21s, you'll realise that you could fit me, Seema and Arlette in that top and still have room to spare. Plus, it was covered in these hideous sequinned leaf-type things. No wonder she left it behind when she went away.

Seema was looking at me and doing these calming hand-type movements. 'That's really kind of you –

isn't it, Magenta?' she said pointedly.

'Yes, it's great,' I said. 'Pity it's the wrong size, though.' Pity? Relief, more like!

'Suit yourself.' Arlette was still being really off with me.

'So, what do you think Magenta should wear to go out with Adam tonight?' I knew Seema was doing her best to make peace.

'Personally, I think anyone who goes out with Adam Jordan should be in a strait-jacket!' Arlette said. Then she raised her voice and shouted at the wall, 'In fact, I think any girl who goes out with any boy should have her head tested!'

Which was all I needed because the music from Daniel's room suddenly increased by a thousand decibels and I couldn't even shout at him to turn it down because I still wasn't speaking to him.

'Well, there's been a bit of a run on strait-jackets,' Seema said, 'so let's see what the options are.'

Seema's so brilliant. But, actually, to be fair to Arlette, I thought it was pretty cool of her to come round. It was nice that it was the three of us again – even if it was a bit strained at times. And that's what I think is so fantastic about being a girl. We're so mature and we don't let silly squabbles get in the way.

Anyway, while we were going through my cupboards, Arlette found these phat pants. I mean, they're not really me – I bought them last year when I was going through a temporary All Saints phase but I'd only worn them once because I bought a pair that were three sizes too big so that they'd sit on my hips and look really cool. The trouble is, last year I didn't really have any hips worth mentioning, so they kept dropping down to my knees and I spent the whole day hoisting them up so that I didn't end up walking down the street in my knickers. I mean, showing off the waistband of your CKs is one thing but when you're revealing rosebud-embroidered BHS Granny's choice, it's so embarrassing. But actually, I've grown now and when I tried them on, they didn't look too bad. In fact, they went fantastically with my fluffy cardigan. They were so long they covered up nearly all my green shoes, which was a pity but I thought, hey I can live with that.

So, at half past five, everything looked wicked: I was going out with the boy of my dreams, my best friend was talking to me again, I was pretty pleased with how I looked – we'd run some glitter through my hair to give it that subtle hint of a sparkle – and Dad had completely backed off and decided to go to some Tai Chi Association meeting in town. I was even considering speaking to Daniel again.

Life was sweet!

But then this weird thing happened: I started to get a bit twitchy about the whole thing. There I was, waiting at the bus stop, imagining us sitting in the cinema; Adam would start by cuddling up to me and then he'd just reach out and let his arm rest round my shoulders. He wouldn't do any of that little boy stuff about pretending to yawn – he'd just come straight out and put his arm round me, like a man. Then, maybe a bit later on, because he wouldn't want to be too pushy or anything, he might lean over and kiss me.

And that's when it happened. This teensy little bit of me started to have a tinge of doubt.

What happened if he kissed me and we got stuck?

I mean, let's face it, my one and only venture into the world of snogging had resulted in five hours in Casualty and a serious mouthal-assault with a pair of pliers. And I'd seen the way Adam and The Pritch had been going at it on the stage at the youth club disco. How could I possibly compete with that? Talk about mega-stress. In fact, by the time I got to the Roxy there was some major self-doubtage going on in my head, which is an entirely new experience for me I can tell you – and not one I'd care to repeat in a hurry.

So, I was sitting on the bus in the middle of this major panic attack when suddenly we went round the corner and he came into view. Oh, he looked so sweet. He was standing outside the main doors and it was like all my worries just floated away. Oh my God, he looked gorgeous. He had his collar turned up and his hands in his pockets and he was looking round like he was waiting for someone. I went all gooey again. And then it dawned on me – he *was* waiting for someone – me!

But by the time I realised it, it was too late. I'd forgotten to ring the bell.

'Oh, stop! Stop the bus! I need to get off!'

I stood up and, although it may have been my imagination, I'm sure the driver accelerated as soon as I shouted *Stop*. Add to that the fact that I'm not completely comfortable with the height of my shoes and my hips hadn't grown into my phat pants quite as much as I'd thought and I was soon having a serious crisis in the clothing department. I ended up toppling sideways along the aisle of the bus like some drunken tap-dancer who was trying to perform on the wobbly walkway in the *House of Fun*. I fell on to the lap of this old man who (completely unreasonably, if you ask me) got very shirty and pushed me away. Then I sort of ricocheted into another man who was reading a paper and accidentally knocked off his glasses, before I ended up in this shopping trolley that was in the luggage compartment. The awful thing was, there was a box of cakes on the top and my hand squelched straight on to it. Most of the cream was on my hand, which was OK because I could lick that off – I just hoped I could delay letting Adam hold my hand until I'd had time to go to the loo and wash properly. I only got a teensy bit of cream on my cardigan, which was a huge relief because I didn't fancy having to do a full clothes wash in the Ladies. But the woman whose cakes they were was not impressed. She seemed to think I ought to pay for them. Honestly – as if I hadn't been through enough trauma!

Anyway, it all turned into a bit of a nightmare, and the bus went sailing straight past the cinema. My first date and I was going to be late!

Of course the next stop wasn't until the centre of town and then I had to decide what to do. Did I wait for a bus going back the other way or walk to the cinema? Why does life have to be so hard? It's all choices, choices, choices! It's bad enough that we're choosing our GCSE options at school but I have to make decisions in my social life as well. But then, wouldn't you just know it – a bus zoomed by on the other side of the road without stopping. Typical! Now I really didn't have a choice so I set off to walk.

Then there was this unfortunate moment when I passed *The Filling Station* and saw Daniel and Spud sitting in the window. I couldn't remember whether or not I was speaking to Daniel again now that Arlette and I seemed to be friends but I knew I definitely wasn't speaking to Sam *The Phantom Menace* Pudmore, so I gave one of those half grin, half snarly type expressions and walked by.

I was getting a bit panicky because it was almost ten past six and I was finding it a bit difficult to walk quickly because:

a) it would be so uncool to arrive all sweaty and breathless, and

b) there was a definite battle for the pavement going on between my shoes and my trousers.

So by the time I got within sight of the Roxy I could see that Adam was a teensy bit peed off. He was sort of kicking his feet and sighing and I was just about to call out to him when who should I see walking towards the cinema from the other direction but Joe and the dreaded Pritch!

'Wazzup?' I heard Joe sneer. 'Been stood up?'

Ggggrrrr! I was a tad furious I have to say but when I saw how Adam handled the situation I went all warm inside. He didn't say anything. Not a thing! He just stared at Joe with one of those looks that would stop a herd of stampeding elephants in its tracks. Oooo, I love the strong, silent type.

'Oh no, I forgot, you've been cradle-snatching from Year 9, haven't you? She's probably had to go home to her babysitter. I mean, it's way past her bedtime.' Then the gruesome twosome both started to giggle. What a cheek! Joe's known me since I was about three and anyway he was talking about Year 9s like we were a whole different generation. I mean, his precious girlfriend's only one year older than I am.

But then Adam made a step towards them and Joe grabbed The Slapper by the arm and they scuttled off into the foyer of the cinema. Wow! I couldn't believe that Adam was being so protective of me. It was like he was defending my honour or something – this was so exciting. I nearly ran the last few steps up to him.

'Hi!' I said. Now don't get me wrong, I was hardly expecting a full on snog, but I did think I might at least get a smile.

'You're late!' Like – whoa! Talk about Mr Tetchy. I mean, I was only ten minutes late – and it wasn't like it was deliberate or anything. 'Come on!' And he turned and walked into the foyer without even giving me a peck on the cheek. And he hadn't said how nice I looked or anything!

And then, would you believe this – he only went and bought one ticket for himself! I mean, I'm as much a feminist as the next girl, but I think it's only reasonable that the boy should pay on a first date. After all, it's tradition, isn't it? But, worse still, he then went off and bought one cup of Coke and one tub of popcorn. I mean, talk about selfish! I was beginning to think that maybe Arlette had been right about Adam – but then I realised he was probably just a bit distracted, what with Joe turning up with his ex and then me being late and everything. The trouble was, I was parched after all that walking but I couldn't really afford a Coke. I've been a bit strapped recently, so Gran had slipped me a fiver but there wasn't much left now that I'd had to pay for my own ticket. Plus, I'd paid full fare on the bus – strictly speaking I'm still a half fare, but you know what it's like. So, anyway, the only thing I could afford was one of those little plastic cartons of orange – you know, the sort you see little kids in pushchairs with. They are so uncool, I had to hide it until we got into the cinema where it was dark. I was starting to get a bad feeling about the whole evening; things were not going the way I'd planned them at all.

The adverts had already started and the cinema was surprisingly full for the early showing, so we got shown to some seats a bit nearer the front than I'd have liked. But honestly, talk about bad luck, guess who was just two rows in front of us? Only Joe and The Pritch! (I could tell by the way the light from the screen was reflecting off her synthetic hair.) I was getting definite vibes of impatience from Adam so I thought I'd try to make him feel a bit better.

'You wouldn't believe the aggro I had getting here,' I said, snuggling up to him a bit – not too much though. I didn't want him to think I was a flirt.

'Really,' he said.

'Ssssh!' someone said from a couple of rows back.

I lowered my voice to a whisper. 'Yes, first of all . . .'

'I'm watching,' he said, stuffing a handful of popcorn into his mouth and moving away from me. I was absolutely gutted – especially as he stayed like that right through the adverts and into the main feature. I wasn't sure what was going on but I felt so miserable. I'd waited such a long time for this and now that awful Anthea Pritchard and the moron from next door were going to spoil it for me. There was a lump in my throat the size of a small boulder but I was determined not to cry. This whole date was a disaster. Adam was scoffing his popcorn and slurping his Coke and sitting about as far away from me as he could get without actually moving into the next seat. And, even worse – Joe and the Slapper were practically eating each other right in front of us! I could feel the tears welling up.

I realised I had two choices:

1) I could either go off to the Ladies and have a good old sob and get it out of my system but end up like the greater red-eyed monster or,

2) I could go for damage limitation and have a sneaky dab with a tissue before the flood gates opened.

No contest really – so it was out with the Kleenex. The trouble was, when I'd bought my ticket I'd put my change in the same pocket as my tissues. So there I was, trying to be discreet and pull them out without Adam noticing, when suddenly there was this clatter of coins. Oh no! Without my money there was no way I could get home because it seemed unlikely that Mr Generosity-Jordan would be up for paying my bus fare. I had to pick up my money.

Now obviously I didn't want to just stand up because that would disturb everyone, so I thought that if I shuffled my bum forward on the seat, I would be able to drop down on to the floor and quietly gather up my money. Of course the one thing that had slipped my mind was how everyone complains that the seats at the Roxy are way too close to the row in front. For starters I had to turn my legs to one side so that I was practically kneeing Adam in the thigh. But then, as my bum slid over the edge and I was poised to slither surreptitiously on to the floor, the seat started to tip up – which would've been fine, except that, somehow my cardigan got hooked over it. So there I was in a sort of twisted half-crouch, feeling like Quasimodo, unable to move. Now, you would've thought that simply undoing the buttons would've solved the problem, wouldn't you? But, oh no – because as I undid my cardigan, the button slipped round between the arm and the seat and got jammed. The next thing I knew, the seat was wedged into the small of my back and I couldn't go either up or down more than about a centimetre. I tried to manoeuvre my knees round to the front so that I could push myself up again but my foot shot forwards and underneath the tiered bit of flooring of the seat in front. I couldn't move it at all and the woman in front kept turning round and giving me dirty looks because my leg kept ramming against the back of her seat. But the other problem was, I'd slipped down so low that the arms of the seat were above my shoulders, which meant that I couldn't use them to lever myself up. I was well and truly stuck – lying there like a beetle that'd rolled on to its back.

'Psssst!' I tried to attract Adam's attention but he was engrossed in the film. 'Oi!' I said, a little louder.

The woman next to me was starting to tut and people were shushing me but Adam seemed to have had a sudden attack of deafness. The first twinge of cramp started to tingle in my calf muscle so I knew that if I wanted to avert a full scale screaming crisis I had to get unwedged – and quickly.

'Adam!' I flapped my arm in his direction, accidentally hitting his tub of popcorn and sending half of it flying.

'Watch it!' he didn't sound too pleased. But then he did a double take. 'What are you doing?'

'I'm stuck.'

He gave this sort of impatient groan. Then he tried to pull me up by one arm but he couldn't manage it. In the end, he had to stand up and ask the guy who was sitting behind us to help him. They took an arm each and yanked until I was free. But honestly, I know there was a lot of seat banging and grunting going on but I have to say the other people in the cinema were not very sympathetic. And the worst thing was, I still hadn't managed to pick up my bus fare.

· I've got to be honest, the whole episode hadn't done much to improve my mood – but I decided to wait until the end of the film when the lights came up so I could find my money. I thought my best bet to get into Adam's good books would be to keep a low profile, so I got out my carton of drink. It had one of those rigid plastic straws that's supposed to penetrate the lid in a special place. Of course, in the pitch dark, I couldn't actually see what I was doing. I had to feel for the raised bit where the straw was supposed to go but it was like the lid was made of reinforced steel, I was pushing and pushing but I couldn't get the straw to go in. 'Mmmmmmrrr.' The effort was enormous. I wondered if the manufacturers had ever thought of selling their product for bullet-proofing the windows of MI6.

'*Now* what's the matter?' He didn't sound too happy but at least I was getting some attention from my supposed date.

'Sssshhh!' came the voice from two rows back.

It was too much. 'Oh, shut up!' I snapped and, as I said it, the straw broke through the lid of my drink. Yes! Success! The trouble was, it seemed to act like a siphon and the orange squash shot up through the straw and into the air. Then it cascaded down, in a sort of a sticky fountain, on to everyone within a three-seat radius.

'Aaagh!'

'What the . . .' People were shouting from every direction. I have to say, I was very surprised at how much those little cartons contain.

Adam leapt up and threw what was left of his popcorn in the air – which didn't exactly help the situation. 'OK! That's it!'

Joe and Anthea Pritchard started jumping up and flapping their arms like it was acid or something. Honestly – it was only a drop of orange drink.

The next thing I knew, torches were advancing on us like a scene from *ET*.

This eerie looking *Blair Witch* character flashed a light at Adam and me. 'Come on, you two. Out!' she barked, like we were criminals or something.

'But it was an accident . . .' I started.

'Out!' she said. Honestly – Gestapo or what?

Then, would you believe it, Adam gave me this prod in the back. 'Just go! Let's get out of here.' Talk about a traitor.

So there we were – it was only seven o'clock and we'd been kicked out of the cinema. I'd got no money left and Adam was dripping in orange. It wasn't quite what I'd had in mind for my first date but, I thought, all was not lost – there were still two hours to go before I had to be home.

'So, where shall we go now?' I asked.

Adam gave me the same look that he'd used for Joe, you know the one that would've turned elephants to stone. 'You have *got* to be joking. *We* are not going anywhere. I, on the other hand am going to hang with my mates – as far away from you as possible!'

And that was it for me. I burst into tears in the middle of the pavement. 'I hate you, Adam Jordan! I'm not surprised Anthea Pritchard two-timed you. You're a . . . you're a . . . selfish, inconsiderate pig!'

And do you know what he did? He just shrugged! 'Whatever!' he said, and walked off across the road. Can you believe it!?

But the worst thing was, I'd only just made up with Arlette and now I was going to have to tell her she'd been right all along. Life is so unfair!

9
Magenta

So there I was, sitting on the wall of *Pasta La Vista Baby*, the Italian restaurant next to the cinema, engaging my brain in some serious lateral thinking and trying to decide how best to deal with my current predicament, when I was rudely interrupted.

'Hi Magenta. Are you all right?' This was all I needed – Archimedes High's answer to Dumb and Dumber. Daniel and Spud.

'I'm fine,' I said. I couldn't remember which one, if either, I was still talking to but to be honest, I didn't care. The two most pressing issues for me at that moment were:

a) how I was going to get home and

b) how I was going to explain what had happened with Adam without looking like, at best, a complete dork and, at worst, a certifiable sociopath.

About a million miles further down my list of priorities there was also the minor issue of trying not to let Daniel and Spud see that I'd been crying.

'Are you crying?' Great! Spud's idea of tact operates on a number of levels – all of them subterranean.

'No!' I said. 'I've just rubbed my eye and got some face glitter in it.' Pretty convincing, I thought, considering my current emotional state.

'What happened to your hair? It looks all wet.' There are occasions when I seriously think someone should rearrange Spud's brace so that the rubber bands go vertically. I mean Sam Pudmore is to diplomacy what Neanderthal man was to rocket science!

Then Daniel got in on the act too. 'We've just seen Adam Jordan. Wasn't it tonight you were supposed to be going out with him?' Like, who did he think he was, Memory-man? Gggrrr!

'Yes, well – I've dumped him.' Strictly speaking, it wasn't a lie because I had said that I hated Adam shortly before he walked off but actually, I just wanted them to cut me some slack.

'You dumped Adam Jordan?' Spud looked impressed. 'Cool!'

I knew that my credibility rating had probably just shot up into the next division but I wished they'd just go away and leave me alone. I looked at my watch. 'Don't you have somewhere to go?'

'No,' Daniel said, sitting down next to me.

'Yes!' Spud looked alarmed. 'What're you doing, Daniel?' Then he grinned that awful wire-mesh grin at me that was a bit too déjà vu for comfort. 'We're going down to @titude to play Quake with the rest of the clan.'

'Cool. Off you go then. Bye!' I know it sounded a bit harsh but I was feeling seriously crowded with all the interrogation about Adam. And if I'm being completely honest, which of course I always am, there was a teensy little bit of me that had hoped Adam might have an attack of conscience and come back for me. Sadly though, I was beginning to realise that that was about as likely as getting Madonna to gig at my dad's birthday party.

Then Daniel had a brain wave – or, at least, it seemed like a brain wave for about a millionth of a second. 'Look, Spud, why don't you go and tell the others that I'm not coming? I'll give you a call in the morning. I'm going to take Magenta home.' Oh, how sweet was that? I suddenly felt really bad about not speaking to him all week.

'Great, I'll help you,' Spud said.

Daniel gave Spud this sort of half slap on the back, half push in the direction of the Internet café. 'I don't need any help, thanks, mate. I'll phone you.' And Spud went off looking a tad miffed. Then Daniel smiled at me in a really concerned way. 'Come on,' he said, 'I'll walk you home.'

'Walk!' Now, call me a couch potato, but walking is not my preferred means of transport at the best of times – and the idea of walking all the way home in my high shoes and with falling-down trousers was about as appealing as going scuba diving in a toxic waste dump. 'Daniel, it's miles.' (Well, maybe that was a slight exaggeration, but it wasn't exactly round the corner either.) 'Can you just pay my bus fare and I'll give it back to you tomorrow?'

He shrugged. 'I haven't got enough – sorry. But if we cut through the park that'll be much shorter.'

Suddenly Spud, with his manic dancing and conversational skills of a parrot, looked appealingly sane. 'Are you mad?' I could not believe Daniel was suggesting going through the park after dark. Apart from anything else, the gates were locked at night and anyway it was home to all sorts of weirdos. 'I may be going out on a limb here, Daniel, but isn't going through the park incredibly dangerous, as well as being illegal?'

'It's OK. Joe and his mates often meet up in there at night.' (I rest my case about the weirdos.) 'He's told me where the fence is broken down – and anyway, I'll be there to protect you – don't worry.'

I have to say, as I'd been sitting on the wall compiling my list of Plans A to Z for getting home, the idea of walking through the park had not even featured – and, believe me, I'd already got up to Plan W. But as nothing else seemed to present itself as an alternative, I decided to trust Daniel – although I have to confess, I wasn't one hundred percent on board with the thought of him as my bodyguard.

We walked a bit further along the road till we came to the bus shelter and then Daniel led me round the back. It was a complete health hazard round there with discarded takeaway cartons and all sorts of rubbish.

'Ugh! This is disgusting, Daniel. I cannot believe I let you talk me into this.'

'It's OK. There's some railing missing along here and then we'll be into the park. Just stay close behind me.' Like I was going to go venturing off on my own!

The way Daniel said it, he made it sound as though after we'd got through the railings it was going to be plain sailing but, actually, it got worse. Behind the railings there was a forest of bushes and things with branches and prickles and all sorts of gross scratchy bits that got stuck in my hair and everywhere.

'Ouch!'

'Ssh!' Daniel whispered. 'We're not supposed to be here, so keep your voice down.' I was getting pretty sick of people telling me to keep my voice down this evening.

My lovely fluffy cardigan was going to be wrecked at this rate and the ground felt grossly squelchy under my feet, so heaven knows what state my shoes would be by the time I got home – if I ever *got* home. Then I heard this ominous scrabbling sound.

'Aaagh! Daniel. What was that?' I grabbed his arm. I think I would rather have crawled home on my hands and knees the long way rather than gone through this. Daniel may get off on all this SAS night manoeuvres stuff, but give me a video and a pizza any day.

'It's probably just a squirrel.'

Yeah, right! I know squirrels. Sirius chases them across the garden and I've seen how they run. That was *not* a squirrel and if Daniel Attenborough thought he could pull the wool over my eyes, he was mistaken. 'It was a rat, Daniel! You've brought me into a rat-infested hellhole. I hate you – get me out of here!'

So he took my hand and led me across the soggy, garden-type bit and on to the path. Dry land – phew! I ran my hand through my hair but it felt like I'd been transformed into a hedgehog – ugh! I dreaded to think what I looked like – thank goodness it was only Daniel I was with.

I have to say, even though we were out of the bushy bit, it still felt a bit creepy in the park – like we were in some parallel universe where we could hear the rest of the world happening but we'd been transported into the twilight zone. I thought that if I ever survived, I'd probably look back on the whole thing and decide that it had really been quite exciting, but right now it was all a bit too scary for my liking. I gave a shudder.

'Are you warm enough? You can borrow my jacket if you like.' Daniel was being so sweet, I had another pang of guilt about not speaking to him.

'Thanks, Dan . . .' I was just about to accept his offer when I thought I heard another noise, only this was too big for either a rat or a squirrel. Eeeek! This was getting really spooky. 'Did you hear something?'

We both stood still and listened.

'Can't hear a thing,' Daniel said, taking off his jacket and putting it round my shoulders. He was so thoughtful I decided to forgive him for taking me through the ratty bit and made a promise to myself never to be horrid to him again.

We went on a bit further but, with no lights in the park, it was getting distinctly eerie in there. Daniel and I were hardly speaking and not because we were peed off or anything – just because we wanted to keep our wits about us. I made a mental note to have another go at Dad about getting me a mobile. He seems to think they're just a brain-frying fashion accessory but they're an absolute necessity. I mean, he's got one and it doesn't seem to have fried his brain – although, come to think of it . . .

'What was that?' It was Daniel's turn to get spooked.

I hadn't heard anything but I grabbed his arm anyway. 'I want to get out of here, Daniel – now!'

'OK. I think I can remember the way.' That came as a bit of a shocker, I can tell you.

'Think? What do you mean you *think* you can remember the way? Don't you know?' Maybe I'd reassess my decision never to be horrid to him again.

'Well, it looks different in the dark and the loose railings on the Park Avenue side aren't as obvious as the others behind the bus shelter.'

'Well, thank you ver—'

Then we both heard it. There was a definite cracking sound, as though someone had trodden on a twig. Ooooooh, this was too scary for words! I could feel my heart beating and I was sure that if it'd been light enough to see, it would've been bouncing out of my chest like something out of a *Loony Tunes* cartoon.

'Run!' Daniel shouted in a sort of whispery way.

Well, it was all right for him, wasn't it! I mean, his trainers were actually made for running but mine only came loosely into the trainer category – whoever designed them had probably never been within a marathon's distance of an athletics track in their life. Running was really not an option for me – and that's even before we talk about the half metre of trouser hem-line that was wrapped round each foot, and the crotch that was swinging between my knees like a khaki hammock. I was just about to protest when I heard definite rustling about ten feet away from us in the bushes.

'OK!' And I hoisted my phat pants as high as I could with one hand, held Daniel's jacket across my chest with the other and just hoped that I'd become acclimatised to my shoes. It wasn't so much a run as a sort of skateless skating action. I don't think Miss Crumm would have even considered me for the relay team but, and I say this with a certain degree of pride, I reckon I might just have managed a personal best to the gates in Park Avenue.

By the time I got there, Daniel had already climbed up the huge wrought iron gates and was sitting astride them. 'Come on, give me your hand.'

'You cannot be serious, Daniel!' He must have been

eight feet off the ground and believe me, I have enough problems with the wall-bars in the gym and they have big squodgy mats under them. There was no way I was even attempting those gates and risking being splattered on the asphalt. 'I thought you said there were some loose railings somewhere.'

'There are but I don't know where. It's quite easy. Come on, I'll help you.'

'Get outta here!' But then there was a weird but definitely human noise, like a cross between a sneeze and a grunt, from over in the shrubbery. 'Help me up!'

I reached up and handed Daniel his jacket, hitched up my trousers and put my foot into one of the curly shaped holes in the ironwork. So far, so good. I even found I could put some weight on that foot while I located another hole for my other foot. Piece of cake, I thought. By this time I could reach Daniel's hand and he was all set to pull me up when – disaster! Try as I might I could not get my foot out of the gate. My shoe had got wedged.

'Go back down and take your shoes off.' Gggrrr! I think an adrenaline surge must have caused some serious brain-leakage on Daniel's part.

'Very helpful, thank you, Daniel. And how do you suggest I get down when I can't move either foot?' I was clinging on, spread-eagled against the gate, unable to move. Some unidentified stalker, maybe even a mass murderer, was lurking in the bushes and, call me melodramatic, but I was beginning to think that Dad's prediction about *Crimewatch* might be coming true. I don't think hysteria has ever been more of a certainty. 'Get me out of here!'

'Wait there.' Humph! Like I had any choice!

But then he jumped down on to the pavement – on the other side of the gates! What was he playing at? 'Don't you dare leave me here, Daniel!'

He'd started to fiddle with my shoes and before I knew what had happened, he'd loosened my laces and pushed my feet out so that I could climb up the gates bare footed. Suddenly, he was back up on top of the gates giving me a hand up. I mean, I've never really thought of Daniel in Superman terms before, but I was dead impressed and felt a bit guilty about thinking he was going to run off and leave me.

When we were both safely on the pavement in Park Avenue, he looked at me with an expression a bit like Sirius when I accidentally tread on his tail, and said, 'I wouldn't desert you, Magenta. They don't call me Adam Jordan.'

Then we both heard this huge kerfuffle in the bushes. It sounded like there was a fight going on with branches swaying and loud voices grunting. Daniel took my hand again. Gosh, he was being so manly; I think he must've been going for the macho award.

'Quick! Let's get out of here!'

'What about my shoes?' Surely he couldn't expect me to leave them stuck in the gate while I ran home in my secret sox?

'Which would you prefer, your life or your shoes?'

It was a tough one, but when he put it that way . . .

Just then, a police car came cruising along on the other side of the road. I mean how lucky is that? So Daniel, who was really taking charge of the situation, ran over and flagged it down.

'Quick – there's someone following us in the park,' he said and before you could say *'Sierra Foxtrot'* they were on the radio calling for assistance. Ooooo, how exciting! The next thing we knew, all these squad cars (well, two) came homing in and directed their headlights on the park gates. It was like something out of *The Bill*! The policemen had a key that unlocked the gate and they went running in with torches while another one asked us some questions. And I have to say, I was a bit shocked at some of the things he was insinuating. He seemed to be suggesting that Daniel and I had gone into the park for a snogging session! As if!

Then, about five seconds later, the ones who'd gone into the park came out again and guess who with? Adam Jordan, no less! In an arm lock! That'll teach him to go off and leave me on my own.

'Magenta! Danno! Will you tell them to get off me?'

'Do you know this lad?' One of the policewomen asked.

I could hardly believe my eyes. 'Adam! What do you think you're doing? You scared the daylights out of us.'

The policeman let him go and he started rubbing his shoulder. 'I got half way into town and then felt really bad about walking off and leaving you, so I came back to try and find you and take you home.' Oh, how sweet is that? I knew Arlette had misjudged him. 'Anyway, I ran into Spud and he told me that you'd set off through the park so I just wanted to make sure you were OK.' I knew he'd come back for me. I knew I should have waited for him instead of letting Daniel talk me into his stupid survival exercise. 'But it's a good job I did too because there was this old geezer in there following the pair of you. He ran off when the pigs – I mean, the police – arrived though.'

As soon as the police officers heard that they went

back into the park to have another look round. The other one kept asking Adam loads of questions about the man in the park but it seems it was probably just some old homeless person.

'Thank you for coming back for me, Adam,' I said, hoping he might suddenly decide to make up for lost time and kiss me.

'Look, Magenta,' he said, taking me to one side. 'I'm sorry I left you on your own. I was pissed off about getting kicked out of the cinema and I wasn't thinking straight. I should never've done it.'

Oh, wasn't he just so considerate? 'That's OK,' I said, going all dreamy again.

'But it ain't gonna happen.'

I hadn't quite caught his drift. 'What isn't?' As far as I could see, it had happened and he'd apologised so we were cool.

'You and me. It ain't gonna happen. We're not going to go out.'

I think I would probably have burst into tears right then and there if Daniel hadn't come up to us.

'Come on, Magenta. They're going to take us home in the police car.'

'But . . .' I looked at Adam.

'You're a sweet kid, Magenta, but . . .' Kid? He'd called me a *sweet kid*! How patronising is that? 'But no way!' Then he pointed a finger at Daniel. 'And if I ever hear you dis me again, Danno . . .'

Then Daniel put his arm round my shoulder and led me towards the police car. 'They've managed to get your shoes out of the gate for you.' But I wasn't really listening. I was tired and fed up and I just wanted to go to bed and cry for a hundred years.

The problem was, although I didn't know it, this was just the beginning of the Saturday night drama.

10
Daniel

Oh wow! Tonight was unbelievable! And who'd have thought it after last week? I mean, talk about hell on a bad day – my life didn't seem worth living. Magenta was refusing to speak to me and Spud, who is supposed to be a mate, kept rubbing it in about how she'd chosen to kiss him and it was merely an accident of orthodontistry they they're still not an item. Plus Adam Jordan, who has the social conscience of an amoeba, asked her to go to the cinema simply so that he could spy on his ex and my scumbag brother. Of course, I couldn't say anything to Magenta about Amoeba-boy because she would've thought I was only saying it because I was jealous. (Which I was – but that wasn't my motive.) Anyway, as it turns out, everything has worked out even better than I could've hoped.

Spud and I were going off to play Quake at the cyber café but, to be honest, he was beginning to get on my nerves with his, 'Ooo, her lips are so soft,' and his, 'all this time you've fancied her but it was me she actually asked to dance.' And then we passed

Adam stomping off down the road like Prince Stompy of Stompville, which I thought was a bit strange as he was supposed to be at the cinema with Magenta. So I began to suspect that things were not going quite as planned when we saw Magenta looking all lost and forlorn on the wall of the pasta place next to the cinema. She looked so cute, like she was just crying out for someone to look after her – and suddenly everything became obvious: my mission (and, believe me, I chose to accept it) was to get her home safely. I could hardly believe my luck.

We walked home through the park and it was so romantic! We held hands and she kept snuggling up to me. I gave her my coat and she pulled it round her shoulders like she really appreciated it. We didn't talk much, but then I always think there are times in a relationship when words just aren't necessary – and this was one of them: it was one of those *companionable silences* you read about in books, you know, when two people are totally comfortable with one another. It was amazing!

And then she got stuck climbing over the gate and I did my Rambo act and rescued her. It was great. Oh, I forgot to mention that we'd heard someone in the bushes so, once we were out of the park, I flagged down a police car – you know, like they do in films.

The police were brilliant and this one who was asking us questions had obviously picked up on the chemistry between us because he gave me this knowing look and part of me was thinking, '*I wish!*' But there was another part of me that was thinking, '*No – I respect Magenta too much to take her into the park for a snogging session.*' I just wanted to get her home safely. Of course the stalker in the bushes turned out to be Amoeba-boy himself and he couldn't even come clean about that: he tried to build up his part and say that there was someone else in there and he was only concerned for her safety. Of course she could see right through him and it seemed to put the final nail in his coffin as far as Magenta was concerned. She was upset, obviously, but I put my arm round her all the way home in the back of the police car. It was brilliant.

But the best bit was, when we got home, Florence, Magenta's gran had gone out. We didn't know where, so I stayed with her. We were in her bedroom, Magenta was sitting on her bed trying to ring her dad on his mobile, but he wasn't answering and I was sitting on the chair next to her dressing table. Suddenly she began to cry.

'He's so horrible, Daniel. I should've seen him for the pig that he really is.'

I handed her a tissue and agreed with her – but not too much. I didn't want to look as though I was gloating. 'My mum always says, it's hard to see the whole person when you're only looking at the bits you like.'

'Oh, that's so true, Daniel. Your mum's so wise.' And then she really really started bawling. Now, I've lived next door to Magenta for ten years and, apart from when she used to fall over when she was a little kid, I'd never really seen her cry – I mean *properly* cry. I always thought that it would be a total turn off. I mean, when Arlette's snotting down the phone (like she has been doing for the past couple of weeks) it's like, beam me up, Scotty. But when Magenta started, I was completely blown away. I just wanted to throw my arms round her and make it all better. The trouble is, while my stomach was doing backflips and my brain was in overdrive, my legs seemed to go into temporary paralysis. I just sat there while she howled. I felt about as useful as a video in a DVD player. 'You're so lucky to have a mum, Daniel. I wish I had my mum!' And off she went again.

Magenta's mum was killed in a car crash when Magenta was tiny – that's why she and Curtis came to live with Florence next door. And most of the time, Magenta's cool about it. She's got a picture of her mum on her wall and everything but she doesn't go on about it. In fact, come to think of it, she hardly mentions her mum. So when she started to say things like that, I didn't quite know what to do.

I tried one of my mum's lines. 'Do you want to talk about it?'

She cried even louder. 'No!'

OK, so I was obviously going down the wrong road with that one. 'How about if I make us a cup of tea?' It never fails on television.

'I don't want a cup of tea.' Sirius had jumped up on to the bed with her and she was cuddling him. I couldn't help feeling a pang of jealousy. 'I want my dad! I want my gran!' I picked up the phone to see if Florence had gone round to her sister's. Magenta was still crying. 'I just want a cuddle.'

Whoa! Were my ears deceiving me? I threw down the phone and went over and sat on the bed next to her. Suddenly it seemed that Magenta's third request was the most pressing.

'It'll be OK,' I said and I put my arm round her. Oh, my God! Do dreams come true or what? She let go of Sirius (who, with only the slightest push from me, seemed pleased to be given the ability to breathe again), and buried her head in my chest. This was a moment to savour forever but I had to be cool – I didn't want to blow my chances. I tried to remember what it was like when I was little and Mum used to comfort me. I put my other arm round her so that she was completely wrapped up in my arms. 'Shhh,' I said softly but there was a part of me inside that was screaming, YEESSS!

'Oh, Daniel, you're so sweet,' she said. Strong or manly would've been better, but I was happy to go with 'sweet'. 'I don't know what I'd've done tonight if you hadn't come along. I'm so grateful.' Grateful was good – I could handle gratitude. I pulled her to me a little more. I could smell her hair – oh, it was so wonderful. 'I'm really sorry I was mean to you last week, Daniel.'

Oh joy! I nestled up to her even closer. She smelled lovely – really exotic. I had another sniff of her hair and was just drifting away on this strawberry-fragranced fantasy when something shot up my nose. I think it must have been some of her hair glitter but whatever it was I could feel it tickling away at the top of my nostril. I tried to twitch my nose to stop the irritation but I could feel the sneeze building up. Oh no! Disaster!

'Achoo!' Sadly her hair glitter was expelled from where it had lodged and returned to its place of origin along with several millilitres of snot. Our moment of tenderness was lost.

'Ugh! Daniel! How gross!'

'Achoo! Achoo!' I couldn't stop.

'Get away from me! You're disgusting!' She was frantically wiping her hair with tissues and going on about how revolting I was when there was the throaty throb of a motorbike outside. Somehow my nasal attack was forgotten and Magenta leapt up. 'Oh, thank heavens – that'll be Gran.'

'What do you mean, that'll be your gran?' I'd failed to connect the pulsating engine noise from outside with my geriatric next-door neighbour – until Magenta put me in the picture.

'This is strictly confidential, Daniel, but Gran and Auntie Venice own this motorbike that they keep in a lock-up near Auntie Vee's flat.' Then she narrowed her eyes and I couldn't help thinking that she'd made a remarkable recovery. 'It's a secret, OK? Break it and I will never speak to you again – understand?'

I've lived next door to Florence long enough to realise that nothing would surprise me about her. So it wasn't just that when most women are getting their bus passes, she had decided to go for the Evil Knievel lifestyle that shocked me, but the fact that Magenta hadn't told me. There was a time when we would've told each other everything. I was a bit hurt, I have to admit. 'How long have you known?'

'A few weeks.' She was running down the stairs.

'So why didn't you tell me? You know I wouldn't say anything.'

'This is strictly on a need-to-know basis, OK? And you didn't need to know. It's simple, Daniel, the more people who know, the more likely it is that Dad might find out.' Then she stopped and looked puzzled. 'I can't imagine what's possessed them to come round on it tonight.' She ran out of the door. 'Gran! Am I glad to see you! But why? I mean, what happens if Dad comes home from his meeting and sees the two of you?'

Florence took off her helmet. She always talks in one long sentence, as though everything's connected. 'Well, that's the whole point, love – hang on a second, Venice, wait till I've got changed and then you can take my gear back over to your place – I won't be a tick – hello, Daniel – Magenta, love, your dad's on his way home but he hasn't been to any Tai Chi meting and the reason why Venice has brought me home on the bike is so that I could get here before he does – there's been a right old to-do.'

'What sort of a to-do?' Magenta looked upset and, to be frank, I'm not surprised. 'Is he all right?'

'I'll be off then, shall I?' I was hoping that they'd

say no because I really wanted to find out what'd happened.

'OK then,' Magenta said – a tad dismissively I thought, considering everything we'd shared that evening – but she was obviously concerned about her dad.

But I didn't get the chance because, just then, a police car pulled up. Now, I just assumed that this was somehow connected with all the fuss in the park (you know, maybe the police had decided to press charges against Adam for stalking us or something), but Florence and Venice obviously knew something we didn't.

'Ooops!' Florence said. 'That's blown it.'

'Uh-oh!' said Venice from the depths of her helmet. 'I said you should've called a cab.'

But then, wait for this – the first person to get out of the police car was Ms Lovell, the Art teacher from school.

'Ms Lovell?' Magenta's jaw was on path-sweeping duty. 'What are *you* doing here?'

But it seemed like Florence and Ms Lovell already knew each other. 'Oh hello, Belinda love – what a going on – I told him not to interfere,' Florence said.

Ms Lovell gave Florence a sort of knowing sigh.

'Er, *hello*! Could someone please explain?' Magenta was in a state of shock.

Then Curtis got out of the police car, looking, I have to say, a bit subdued. 'Thank you, officer and, as I said, I'm sorry for the inconvenience.' But when he turned round and saw Florence in her leather gear, it was like someone had pressed the detonator and he exploded. 'What the . . . Mother!'

'Don't you *Mother*, me, Curtis Orange – at least I'm not the one rolling up in a police car!'

I thought it would be discreet of me to leave the proceedings at this point. 'Well, I'll be off then, shall I? Night, Magenta . . .'

'Oh no you don't!' Curtis turned on me. 'I want to speak to you – inside!' From the tone of his voice I just knew that he didn't want to speak to me in a good way.

'Let's all keep calm, shall we?' Ms Lovell said. And then it dawned on me – Ms Lovell had told me that she did Tai Chi as well, so she'd obviously been at the same meeting as Curtis, although why they were coming home in a police car was still proving a bit of a stretch for my imaginative powers.

'How . . . ? Why . . . ?' Magenta was standing by the gate in a state not too far removed from that of a boxer who's just been counted out. 'I . . . don't . . .'

She seemed incapable of speaking in more than single words. 'What . . . ?'

'Inside! All of you!' Visibility was not good under the streetlights but I'm pretty sure that the veins on Curtis's forehead were pulsating alarmingly. Ms Lovell had said that her Tai Chi was a spiritual thing, but the way Curtis was behaving he seemed about as spiritual as some medieval torturer. In fact, things were fast turning into a scene from Jerry Springer.

'I think we'd better go inside,' I said and put my arm round Magenta's shoulder to lead her back indoors.

'Take your hands off my daughter!' Curtis lunged at me with a passable attempt at the world long jump record.

Eeek! I snatched my hand away from Magenta as though she'd spontaneously combusted. Call me a coward, but I couldn't see how dying a slow painful death at the hands of a demented parent could possibly help my quest for the girl I loved.

Once the police car had driven off, we all sat round in Magenta's sitting room like the final scene from a murder mystery. Ms Lovell appointed herself the only objective person in the room so she led the proceedings. She's great. I think she's cool – although it still wasn't clear how she'd got involved in the whole episode.

The first shocker of the evening was when Curtis fessed up to being the mysterious stalker in the park. It turns out that he'd been having dinner in the Italian restaurant next to the cinema so that he could keep an eye on Magenta. When he'd seen the two of us go off into the park he followed us to make sure she was OK. The only snag was, he'd gone and got himself arrested in the process and (for some reason that wasn't obvious at that stage), had phoned Ms Lovell to go to the police station and vouch for his good character.

'How could you?' Magenta cried. 'You don't trust me, do you?'

'Of course I trust you.' I'll give Curtis his due, he did look a bit shame-faced but, to be honest, he wasn't convincing me, let alone his own daughter.

'Oh yeah! Like, how is trailing me on a date trusting me, Dad?' My ears pricked up – she was calling our walk through the park a *date*! Wow! This was excellent progress.

'Your dad does trust you, love,' Florence chipped in.

But Curtis rallied with a swift dig at his mother's bid for independence. 'We'll come to your part in all this later, Mother!' There were times when I had to feel sorry for the guy – I mean, you couldn't really say that either his mother or his daughter was particularly low maintenance, could you? But I was going for the *keep-your-head-down* means of survival and remained schtum.

'I explained to your father that you'd be OK as long as you were with Daniel,' Ms Lovell added. I allowed myself the beginnings of a smile. 'I told him how responsible Daniel is, and how trustworthy.' But somehow, the more she went on the less these seemed like admirable qualities and more like a death sentence on my street-cred. 'I said to him, if she's going to be safe with anyone, she'll be safe with Daniel.' Humph! Safe, am I? Well she obviously didn't see the way I scaled those gates and rescued Magenta from the clutches of what could well have been a mad axe-man.

Magenta looked totally spaced out by all this. Then she turned to Ms Lovell and said, 'What I don't get is, why did he call you? I didn't even know you *knew* my dad – except for parents' evenings and stuff like that.'

And then – wait for this – Ms Lovell looked at Curtis, who looked at Florence, who looked at Venice and they all shrugged like everyone knew something but no one knew what to say. Then Curtis went over and took Magenta's hand like he was breaking bad news or something. 'Darling . . .'

Magenta leapt up as though she'd been stung. 'Oh no, you don't! You only ever call me *darling* when you're going to say something you know I won't like.' Which is true, actually. My mum's just the same.

But anyway it turns out that Curtis and Ms Lovell have been an item for about six months! I mean, how mind-blowing is that? It seems that they met at Tai Chi class and started going out before they knew that Ms Lovell was Magenta's teacher. When they worked it out she wanted Curtis to come clean with Magenta but he didn't want to and it all went a bit pear-shaped for a few weeks. And tonight, Ms Lovell had suggested meeting up to talk about what they were going to do, whether they were going to finish, or break the news to Magenta and try to make a go of it. Curtis had decided that they could kill two birds with one stone: if they went for dinner at the Italian place he could track Magenta at the same time as they sorted out their relationship! Very smooth thinking on Curtis's part, I thought.

Well, of course, you can imagine how Magenta reacted when all this came out.

'No! You can't be!' The strange thing was, she

seemed to be more angry with Ms Lovell than she was with Curtis. 'How could you? He's old enough to be your father!'

'That's not strictly true, Magenta. I'm twenty nine, so there's a ten year age gap and I don't think that's unreasonable.'

'Well, he hasn't got a ponytail or rainbow jumpers or anything!' I wasn't sure what she was going on about and it did seem as though she'd lost the plot a bit but then her bottom lip started to go. 'I thought you liked me.'

'I *do* like you, Magenta,' Ms Lovell said, and then she smiled this lovely smile at Curtis, 'and I also love your dad.'

Wow! Talk about romantic – I went all gooey inside when she said that but Magenta burst into tears again. She went to walk out of the room but she stopped and said, 'I hope you realise that he eats beefburgers!' And then she stomped upstairs.

No one said anything for a while but all the women were looking at Curtis, doing a silent 'I-told-you-so'. He rolled his eyes in this 'OK, OK' sort of way and sighed. 'All right, I'll go and talk to her,' he said.

Ms Lovell beckoned him back. 'Why don't you let Daniel go?' Oh – YES! I love this woman!

I stayed with Magenta till my mum came round looking for me at about eleven o'clock. It was amazing. She was going on and on about the humiliation and I just held her while she cried and gave her tissues when she needed to blow her nose – it was so romantic. In fact, the whole of tonight has been probably the best time of my life (even better than when Mum took us to that holiday camp when I was seven and I won the 'Master Universe' competition and Joe didn't even get into the final). Wow! I just keep putting my memory on rewind.

The only thing that's niggling me a little bit is that Ms Lovell said I was 'safe, reliable and trustworthy'. I mean, that's OK if you're applying for a Saturday job but it's hardly pulling power material, is it? So, I'm lying here looking up at Sarah Michelle and listening for any noise from next door and thinking to myself that perhaps it's about time I got a new image. Daniel Davis is about to become seriously dangerous!

11
Magenta

OK – things which are totally unbelievable and yet, apparently, true:

1) Of all the unmarried women in the world my dad has chosen to go out with one of my teachers.
2) My favourite teacher (who had led me to believe that she was totally cool until a couple of weeks ago) has completely taken leave of her senses and is going out with a balding, middle-aged, single parent who has absolutely nothing in common with her except that they're both into Tai Chi. (And, to be totally fair, my dad is a bit arty – well, he's a graphic designer so I suppose that counts.)
3) Both of the above have got into collusion with the Great Pink Blob and I'm on report until the end of term.
4) It's almost the end of term – they say time flies when you're having fun, but I'd hardly call this term a bundle of laughs.

And:

5) Seema has finished with Ben and is going out with

Hayden West, Arlette is going out with Ben and I'm the only one without a date for the Christmas party on Friday!

Now – things which are totally believable and are true: Life sucks!

Honestly, just when I thought my life had hit rock bottom it was suddenly, 'Grab the miners' lamp because we're heading for the centre of the Earth!'

At home the atmosphere is about as welcoming as a freezer in the Arctic. Dad and Gran have reverted to the Neolithic method of communication: grunting only when necessary. Gran is making a bid for the premier league of women's rights and is even riding the Flo-mobile to Tesco's – which gets up Dad's nose more than the pollen count. Ms Lovell comes round quite a lot, which I find so embarrassing. I mean, let's be honest, if Dad was going to go out with one of my teachers you'd think he could at least have chosen someone who could be used to my advantage – like Mrs Blobby for instance? (Although on second thoughts, maybe not!) As it is, Ms Lovell was just about the only one who liked me and now people will say that it's only favouritism. And that's thrown all my options into a complete mess because Art was about the only subject I really wanted to take.

Although, don't even start me on the subject of Options. I mean, what a joke! I actually looked up the word in the dictionary because I got summoned to an interview with *mein Fuhrer*, Mrs Blobby. It means: *the act of choosing or deciding; the liberty to make choices*. Yeah! Right! Like there's any liberty at all on the part of the student! For a start, the government's chosen six of the nine subjects – so there's a whole heap of liberty there, isn't there? And as for the others, to be honest, I think The Crusher could be done under the Trade's Descriptions Act because the only choices I can see are those of the teachers choosing who they *don't* want in their classes next year.

Mrs Hideous-in-pink sat there tapping her fingers looking at my Options form with my favourite subjects ticked: Art, Textiles and Sociology (I'm not sure what Sociology is, but it sounded really intellectual). 'The problem is, Magenta . . .'

Problem? No one else seemed to have had a problem with their Options.

'The staff want to see some element of commitment before they accept students on to their GCSE courses.'

I was shocked. 'Oh, believe me, Mrs Bl . . . Delaney, I am totally committed.' (I mean, if Billy O'Dowd, the delinquent of the year who has taken *behavioural difficulties* to a whole new dimension, has shown enough commitment to be accepted on to his choices, then why was there any question about *my* commitment?)

'I suppose, really, it's a question of how one would define the term *commitment*.' She peered at me over the top of her latest carbuncle. 'You see, simply turning up to a lesson so that you can make fatuous remarks . . .' (Fatuous – another good word to make a note of and drop into conversation casually. I wasn't sure what it meant but it sounded impressive.) '. . . and seldom handing in homework, does not constitute commitment for the majority of staff at Archimedes High.'

Ouch! A little harsh, I thought, but perhaps not a good time to argue. I was more likely to get what I wanted if I played the *I've-seen-the-error-of-my-ways* card.

'I know, Mrs Delaney.' I tried to look contrite. 'This hasn't been a good term for me.' I looked up to check whether or not she was actually looking at me but she had that impatient, *I've-seen-it-all-before* look on her face. I took out a tissue and blew my nose. 'I've been having a few problems at home.' Which was true. In fact, I'm surprised I'm still sane to be honest with you. I dabbed my eyes as though I was holding back the tears.

'It won't wash with me, Magenta. I've spoken to your father at great length so I know exactly what's been going on at home.'

Parents – honestly!

The good news is that I got the go ahead for Textiles but was vetoed on the Sociology front. However, in Mrs Blobby's words, 'after some persuasion', Mr Kingston had agreed to let me start Geography (which, on my one to ten of choices, was somewhere in double figures.) But, wait for this – on condition that I sign a written contract at the beginning of the course and with the proviso that he reassesses my commitment after one term. Honestly! And I thought Mr Kingston was so cool. It just shows you – there he is playing at being Mr Trendy-lefty-I-love-my-students, when in actual fact, he's like Vlad the Impaler in denim! You just can't take people at face value these days.

Which leaves me with one other choice. The irony is that I was practically guaranteed an A* in Art, but now Ms Lovell's gone and screwed it all up by putting herself forward as my wannabe step-mother. There's no way I can take it now. So that limits my options to either Economics (which has never really been my strong point – even on the pocket money front), or Music – and, to be honest, I wouldn't know an A sharp from a B flat, so I think that's a bit of a no-no as well. Arlette and Seema were no help at all – in fact they even sided with Mrs Blobby and said I should do Art anyway, but ask to be in someone else's group. To be fair to our venerable head of year, she has given me until January to think about it.

But when I tried to talk to Daniel about it he started going all weird. Come to think of it, he's been acting very strangely since the night he walked me home through the park. The first thing, right, is that Daniel has had floppy hair for ages. When I say *floppy*, I don't mean as long as Spud's (who is starting to look scarily like the guy off *Changing Rooms*) but Daniel's was definitely nearer to Hugh Grant than David Beckham. And he took real pride in it too – to be honest there were times when I thought he was worryingly girlie about his hair. Sometimes, when I was round at his, I'd watch him in front of his mirror combing and brushing it. And (I never told anyone else this) there were times in the morning when I could hear a hairdryer through the wall, so I know that he used to blow dry.

Then, one evening a couple of weeks ago, I went

over the balcony to talk to him and nearly jumped out of my skin.

'Aaaagh!' There was this stranger in Daniel's bedroom.

'What's up?' The person who came to the French window had familiar features but I was having real difficulties placing him.

'Daniel? What's happened to you? Has someone stolen your hair?'

'Ha ha ha. Very funny, Magenta! It's called re-creating myself.' Then he just walked back into his room. He didn't look pleased to see me or anything.

I know Daniel and I have been through a bit of a rough patch, what with the Arlette business, but I thought we'd got through that – especially after he was so sweet about walking me home. And he'd been really supportive with the whole Dad and Ms Lovell fiasco, so I was a bit miffed to get such a cool reception – plus, he hadn't even asked my opinion about having his hair cut. And then, get this, he went over to his mirror and started running wax through his hair till it was standing up like a reinforced toilet brush.

'What do you mean, re-creating yourself? People of our age don't re-create themselves. You're not Geri Halliwell, you know!'

'Look, Magenta, I'm really busy at the moment, did you want something?'

Honestly, the cheek of it! 'Not really – I just wanted to talk abut my entire future but it wasn't important. I'll make an appointment next time.'

So that's it in a nutshell – my two best friends are both *in lurve* and may as well have had frontal lobotomies for all the intelligent conversation I get out of them. My dad is *in lurve* and wanders around looking as though he's having a permanent dreamfest – until he meets Gran and then he looks like Sirius with indigestion. School is like Alcatraz, and Daniel seems to have reinvented himself as Gel-Boy – the hard man of hair mousse! And on top of all that it's the Christmas party on Friday and I've nothing to wear and no one to go with.

What is it about school parties? They always miss the mark. Like this was supposed to be an upper school Christmas Extravaganza for Years 9, 10 and 11, but what that means in reality is a feeble little jig about for most of Year 9, about half of Year 10 and only the few of Year 11 who didn't have anything else more interesting to do – like watching television or revising for their mocks. (And that included Joe, of course, who spent the whole time in the corner with Ms Comatose, probably trying to decide whose turn it was to have the brain cell.) Honestly, I think Mrs Delaney needs to take party-planning lessons from Bruno the youth leader because this was seriously bordering on the funereal.

For a start it was only from six till nine, which is hardly burning the midnight oil, is it? Something about the teachers wanting to get home to be with their families after a hard day at work – honestly! Plus, there was no DJ, only taped music and I think the lighting was courtesy of Her Majesty's Prison Service. It was either full-on fluorescent or semi-darkness with the lights from the girls' toilets and a string of fairy lights that Ms Lovell had donated, bringing a hint of illumination to one end of the hall. Earlier on there seemed to be a power struggle going on between Mrs Delaney and Mr Onanije, the deputy head, as to whether to go for the glaring daylight effect or the vaguely festive gloom. So, it was a bit like trying to dance in a thunderstorm – one minute we were lit up like it was midday in August and the next we were groping about falling over each other in the half-darkness. Fortunately Mr Onanije won and we ended up with the fairy lights so there was marginally more atmosphere than a launderette on Saturday night.

I spent most of the time dancing in a group with Chelsea Riordan and Hattie Pringle – the only other cool singles in the whole place. Hattie's just split with her boyfriend, Max, from Year 10 and Chelsea's going out with someone from Leonardo da Vinci, so he wasn't allowed to our school's do. Now, I'm not saying that everyone else was in couples, because they weren't. In fact, to be fair, it was probably about half and half, but it seemed that all the best people were already paired up – except for Hattie, Chelsea, and me, of course. I began to seriously wonder what had possessed me to go, but then I remembered that I'd gone because Seema and Arlette had asked me to. I sometimes think I take my responsibilities as a friend too far.

Daniel was there and he did acknowledge me but he seemed to have a constant circle of girls round him. I don't know if his mum's bought him some new after-shave or what, but I can't say I go a bundle on this re-creation of himself. He hardly even speaks to me any more. I mean, you'd have thought that living next door to each other we could've walked here tonight, wouldn't you? But oh no! He was too busy getting ready when I called round.

'I'll see you there,' he called out. He couldn't even be bothered to come to the French windows and speak to me face to face. Then he turns up at about half past seven and anyone would think Robbie Williams had walked through the door. Honestly, he needs to get over himself if you ask me.

Anyway, I was getting majorly bored by the whole evening. Arlette was in a full-on tongue tickling session with Ben, and Seema and Hayden West had gone into competition with them. I mean, don't get me wrong, I like Chelsea and Hattie, but they're both boffins – cool boffins, but boffins nevertheless and I'm not really into that whole pumping neurones thing at the moment. I mean, there'll be plenty of time for that when I'm older. So I decided to go off to the loo and reassess my situation.

Why is it that there's always a queue in the girls' loos? It doesn't matter where they are; school, or the shopping centre or the cinema. Women can be standing there cross-legged and they still have to wait in line for half an hour like toilets are going out of style. Boys never have to queue – it's so unfair. Anyway, there was no way *I* was going to queue up when all I wanted was some peace and quiet to reflect on this evening and my life in general, so I went down the corridor to the ones in the maths block.

Bummer! There was a cone outside the door and a notice saying:

Typical! I'd only used them that afternoon and they hadn't needed any repair work then. Life really did seem to have it in for me. But then I noticed a light shining from under the door. I gave it a little push and it opened – yes! My luck finally seemed to be changing.

There wasn't any sign of building work going on but, to be honest, all the toilets in our school are a disgrace. Anyone would think they'd been built out of cardboard they're so flimsy and there's graffiti all over the walls, so if they are rebuilding them, it isn't before time. The door of the first cubicle was closed and I assumed that someone was in there, so I went in the last one and sat down to give some serious thought to my plan of action. I couldn't help thinking that this was becoming a bit of a habit – spending social events sitting in toilets.

Should I stick it out for the last hour, I wondered, or just cut my losses and go home now? I mean, I hadn't even seen anyone worth going after. There was a lot of talk about this new boy in Year 10 who had been excluded from Leonardo da Vinci and started a couple of weeks ago but I'd never actually set eyes on him. Adam Jordan wasn't there – thank goodness! I'd been avoiding him for the last few weeks. I didn't think I could face him after the episode in the cinema. I'll admit it was pretty dim in the hall but I couldn't see anyone else who was remotely fanciable, so I was pretty resigned to the fact that there was no way I was going to get lucky – again! The whole evening was more than a tad disappointing and I was feeling pretty depressed about the whole thing when I looked up and, on the wall just above my head, saw:

I ♥ Daniel Davis

Now, it hadn't been *that* long since I'd been in that particular cubicle so I knew this must've been a relatively recent addition to the décor, and couldn't be related to Arlette's minor brainstorm at half term. Surely there couldn't be *two* people who fancied Daniel?

Just then I heard some other girls come in – couldn't they read the sign? This was supposed to be out of bounds.

'Oh my God! He is so gorgeous since he's had his hair cut.'

'I know!'

Of course they could've been talking about anyone, so I was only half listening really.

'Talk about fit!'

190

Then I heard a third person come in and my ears pricked up.

'Hi Anth! How's it going with Joe?'

'Great, thanks – he's so sweet.'

Sweet? Anthea Pritchard was describing Joe Davis as *sweet*! Yeah, right! About as sweet as a pickled gherkin. I was just about to get annoyed about having my privacy invaded when their conversation started to get really interesting.

'And what about his brother?' And they all giggled! I suddenly felt very protective towards Daniel. How dare they make fun of him behind his back!

'He's soooo lovely!' said the first voice.

'Shame he's only Year 9 though, don't you think?'

What was this? It seemed that they weren't making fun of him after all. I was beginning to think that I'd accidentally stumbled on some secret Daniel Davis Admiration Society. Curiosity was beginning to get the better of me. I didn't recognise either of the voices apart from The Pritch's and yet it was clear that they both had the hots for Daniel – my Daniel! I bent down to try and look under the door and see who they were but all I got was an eyeful of ankles – not the most easily identifiable piece of anatomy. I thought that maybe I could get a sneaky look at them through a crack in the doorframe but these loos have been built out of those slot-together pieces and the way the doors are hinged means there isn't a crack to look through. But, if I climbed up on to the loo, I would probably be able to surreptitiously peek over the door. I didn't want to be seen so, instead of putting my hands over the top, I pressed them against the sides of the cubicle while I stepped up on to the seat. It didn't feel terribly stable but I'm afraid that my inquisitiveness had gone beyond the point of no return.

I was standing on the loo with my knees bent so that my head was below door height, but craning my neck so that I could just snatch a quick look. I just hoped they weren't looking in the mirrors and wouldn't catch a glimpse of me. But, would you believe it, I was just about to pop my head up when someone else came in! It was busier than Trafalgar Square on New Year's Eve in there! Couldn't a girl do a spot of eavesdropping without the whole world getting in on the act?

'Hi Kerry.' Kerry? That could well be Kerry Pudmore, Spud's sister, who was the total opposite to Spud. First of all she was really pretty but also, Sam's a fairly placid sort of guy whereas Kerry has a temper like a pre-menstrual volcano. 'Was that Ryan, the new boy, you were chatting up?'

'What if it was?'

The others backed off. 'Nothing. Just wondered.'

'Emma's going to ask Daniel Davis out.' Emma? I could think of at least five Emmas, so I was none the wiser.

'No chance,' I heard Kerry say.

'In your dreams, girl,' The Slapper added.

'Why not?'

'Cos everyone knows he fancies Kerry's brother's ex,' Anthea said.

'That's, like, last century's news,' Kerry sneered.

Daniel fancies Spud's ex? He hadn't told me. Honestly I was beginning to wonder what had happened to my friendship with Daniel – first of all he didn't consult me about having his hair cut and then he gets the hots for someone and doesn't talk to me about it. I needed to have a serious talk to him over the holidays. But then I realised Spud doesn't have an ex. In fact, the closest he's ever been to going out with anyone was the unfortunate, best relegated to the memory-dungeons, never to be referred to in the history of the Universe, episode at the youth club dance – with me.

Oh my God! People couldn't possibly be thinking of me as Spud's ex, could they? Think what that would do for my reputation! I really needed to see who these girls were so that I could put them straight. But then another vital piece of information began to filter through. She'd said that everyone knew that Daniel fancied Spud's ex. And if she was referring to me as Spud's ex, that means that everyone knew Daniel fancied me! Everyone except me, that is. I was in a state of shock.

Could it really be true that Daniel fancied me? Wow! I mean, I've never really thought of him like that before. This put our friendship in a whole different context because I didn't fancy him – or did I? I mean, I suppose I did feel a teensy bit jealous when he was going out with Arlette. And it was nice when he walked me home through the park that night. And he did look quite cute with his hair short. Mmm – it was certainly worth thinking about.

'Not the one with the brace?' one of the unidentified girls said – and I have to say, I didn't like the tone of her voice.

'Meaning?' I suddenly remembered that Spud and Kerry weren't quite total opposites – there was a definite similarity in the dental region.

'Nothing.'

'We didn't mean anything, Kerry, honest.'

There was a heated argument about whether the two girls had meant to insult Kerry (who, I have to confess, was going up in my estimation as she defended the silent minority of the brace-wearing public).

'Just bog off, Emma!' I heard her go into the cubicle next to the one I was in – or should I say, I *felt* her go into the loo next to mine because she slammed the door pretty hard. In fact, so hard that it apparently bounced open again. The walls were shaking rather alarmingly with the force of it all so I decided to get down off the loo seat. As I looked down on the floor I saw a small pile of shiny metal objects and a screwdriver by the side of the toilet. I couldn't make out what they were at first.

'OH!' Kerry shouted in frustration. It sounded as though she gave the door a violent kick and there was the tinkling sound of metal falling on to a hard surface. There was a horrible moment of realisation when I saw a gleaming silver screw rolling across the toilet floor – identical to the ones that were heaped up with the screwdriver just under where I was balanced. I was still on top of the toilet with my hands pressed up against the sides and I could feel them reverberating every time she slammed the door. My eyes did a quick scan of the cubicle and I felt sick. There was not one single screw left in any of the joints.

The next twenty seconds seemed to last a decade. The wall between Kerry and me began to collapse away from me. My weight was pressed against it and I could feel myself toppling sideways. I knew I needed to get down off the toilet seat, so I reached forward and grabbed for the door to steady myself. Unfortunately, as the side panel caved in on Kerry's head, the front panel fell forwards with me spread-eagled against it. It collapsed in a sort of ripple effect along the length of the four cubicles with bolts pinging loose and joints coming apart in a Mexican wave. On the way down the hand drier that had been attached to the wall went flying, getting catapulted into the sink and knocking off the hot tap. Water began to spurt everywhere. And, almost simultaneously, as the front of the loos fell away, the side walls fell over in a domino effect until only the end cubicle was left – swaying precariously. It teetered momentarily, then fell, exposing Janet Dibner sitting on the fourth loo with her knickers round her knees and looking as though she'd just wandered out of a war zone.

For several seconds there was a sort of eerie silence with only the squirting of water and some muted whimpering from Janet Dibner about being killed by Mrs Delaney because no one else was supposed to be in there. It seems that she had a bit of an upset tummy so Mrs Blobby (showing no favouritism whatsoever) had given her the key but told her not to allow anyone else in.

Then all hell seemed to break loose. Kerry was screaming that the wall had hit her on the head. Anthea, Emma and the other girl (who turned out to be Shanti Wray in Year 10) were screaming – totally unjustifiably, in my opinion, I mean, it's hardly major trauma getting a bit wet from an exploding tap! But perhaps the loudest and (considering the amount of pain I was in) the most valid scream was from me. My fingers had been clasping the top of the door when it hit the floor and, although there was a bit of a gap because the door was inset slightly, they'd taken the brunt of the impact and were being transformed into huge purple sausages in front of my eyes.

Suddenly the whole toilet area was filled with people; teachers, pupils, girls, boys, the caretaker. The next few minutes were a bit of a blur, really.

'Clear the area,' Mr Onanije was shouting.

'The emergency services will be here shortly,' I heard Mrs Blobby saying.

'Magenta!' Daniel was outside.

And then I heard Ms Lovell's voice. 'It's OK, Samson. Let him through.'

I struggled to sit up. My hands were throbbing but I was pretty sure nothing was broken. Poor old Janet was still sitting on the loo in a state of undress. 'Don't let him in,' she was crying.

But Emma and Shanti both gasped and went all pathetic. 'Hi Daniel.'

I staggered to my feet. I was feeling distinctly wobbly and Daniel came straight up to me and put his arm round my shoulder. The tap was gushing water at the ceiling and it was splashing down as though we were in a shower, so all of us were beginning to look as though we'd just got out of a swimming pool, with hair plastered to our heads and mascara half way down our cheeks.

But Daniel didn't seem to notice. 'Are you all right?' I was touched by the concern in his voice. I began to run through some of the things I'd overheard. Could it be true that he'd fancied me for ages? Was he really as gorgeous as the others were saying? I looked at him again and, I have to say, he did look dangerously attractive. How could I not have noticed? 'What're you looking at?' he asked.

I felt ridiculously embarrassed and didn't know

what to say, so I stalled. 'Erm . . .'

Then Kerry, who was still rubbing her head, kicked aside the piece of wall that had landed on her. 'Oh, just kiss him, for heaven's sake and put us all out of our misery!'

So I did!

And, oh wow! You would not believe what a fantastic kisser he is! I felt like a whole herd of butterflies was stampeding through my tummy. I could feel his arms round me pulling me closer – it was amazing. I would've liked to have put my arms round him too but my hands were still pulsating painfully, so I just sort of squeezed him between my elbows and hoped that he understood.

'About bloomin' time!' I heard Anthea Pritchard say and I decided to review my opinion of her – maybe she wasn't so awful after all.

We seemed to be kissing for ages and, I have to admit, I didn't want the kiss to end. It was just so amazing. But then this strange thing happened. I started to get a funny taste in my mouth. It was sort of a soapy taste and it was getting stronger. In fact, it was getting so strong that in the end I had to pull away.

'What the . . . ?' Daniel had suds and bubbles frothing up all over his head and running down his entire face. I was horrified. It seemed as though I'd only just discovered the boy of my dreams and now he was going to dissolve before my very eyes.

'Grrr! I'm going to kill my brother.' It turns out that Joe had run out of hair wax so had taken Daniel's and used it all up. When I'd called round for him they'd been in the middle of a humungous row about it but anyway his mum had used the potato peeler to shave off some flakes from a bar of soap and had used them to mould Daniel's hair into shape. 'You'll be OK because the weather forecast says it's going to be dry,' she'd told him, 'but at the first spot of drizzle you'd better get yourself an umbrella or you'll turn into a pumpkin.'

I put my arms round his neck and used my elbows to pull him close. 'Well, Daniel Davis, you can be my soapy pumpkin any time.' And I kissed him again.

P.S.

So, we're sitting here in the hall waiting for the ambulance. Mrs Blobby's sent everyone home but Daniel's said he wants to come with me, which is just so lovely of him. Ms Lovell went and got us all blankets and towels from the Home Economics department and we're snuggling up close. It's so romantic. Of course it would be even more romantic if we could hold hands but my fingers are like a pound of plums so that's not really an option. It doesn't matter though, because Daniel's put his arm round me instead and my head's resting on his shoulder. Ooo, this is so wonderful. I can't believe things have turned out so well.

It was all a bit scary in there for a while but fortunately no one's seriously hurt – only poor old Janet Dibner's pride and my fingers really. And I've totally revised my opinion of both Anthea Pritchard and Kerry Pudmore. There's Kerry now, over by the door. I wonder who that is she's talking to? I don't remember seeing him around – unless it's the new boy they were all talking about – the one who's come here because he's been excluded from Leonardo da Vinci.

Wow – no wonder everyone's raving about him. He is *so* gorgeous. Now that's what I'd call one seriously fit individual! I wonder if he lives near me? I must phone Arlette and Seema – as soon as I get the use of my fingers back . . .

Writing
MAGENTA ORANGE was
great fun. And, alarmingly, I
didn't have to search very far to come
up with ideas for some of her antics – my
own family supplied more than enough of those!
The hardest part of writing MAGENTA ORANGE
was getting inside the different characters'
heads and viewing the same situation from
different perspectives. It was also the
most interesting part. Maybe Magenta
will learn to see things from other
people's points of view
one day? We'll see!